Abou

This is a fast moving plot with clandestine night raids in north west Scotland. Some locations are based on geographical features; for example the *Great Stack of 'Sanday'* was first climbed by Graeme Hunter, Douglas Lang and the author.

It is a tale of adventure, danger, mountains and sea; of Templar, Treasure, which is not that far fetched. The writer has taken expeditions into the Upper Amazon in search of Inca treasure but found only adventure and danger, others went mad. The Templar Hoard also has convincing leads.

The central characters are two Special Forces officers, who with a glamorous marine archaeologist discovered searching for Treasure Trove was not without risk. High tech stealth equipment was deployed to thwart an opposition with ruthless aspirations.

Much research was done compiling this book to provide a logical plot for a nail biting saga.

First published in 2011
by Glencoe Productions Ltd.,
Glencoe, Argyll, Scotland

ISBN: 978-0-9514380-2-2

Printed in Scotland by
Bell & Bain Ltd., Glasgow

Typeset in 11 point Sabon
by 3btype.com

Errant Nights

HAMISH MACINNES

Glencoe Productions Ltd.
Glencoe, Argyll,
Scotland PH49 4HX

Dedication

In memory of
Dr. Susan Richards and Douglas Lang,
both killed separately in the mountains.
Sue made the only long rope traverse onto the
Great Stack of Handa, (Sanday).
Douglas was on the first ascent. Much earlier,
a local fisherman, Alasdair Munro, went under the
stack in a rowing boat.

—O—

Prelude

Jack Rippon got lifted with the swell which was pulsing from the north west on to a rock studded with barnacles. He pushed up his face mask and leaned back on his two air cylinders, rejoicing in gulping the pure salty air. Both fins dangled in the waves. His rib was tethered round the corner of the hundred metre red sandstone cliff in a sheltered geo. To the north west the Atlantic reached to infinity in parallel white bandings. He was feeling tired after diving at the adjoining rock stack, equal in height to the cliff itself and of prodigious girth. His black dry suit merged with dark kelp, draped like a plaid over the lower edge of the rock. He took in the wild watery scene. Suddenly, he was alert; he heard engines, the deep, highpowered throb of twin outboards despite the fact that they were barely ticking over. This is what made him nervous. It wasn't just the stirring sea at this dangerous end of the Island of Sanday: adventure tourists wouldn't be taking in this cliff line in such weather. They would have scuttled to the safety of one of the sea lochs which indent the mainland coast just a short distance away. In any case, he hadn't seen a human all day when he had surfaced. Dusk and a storm were imminent.

The menacing dark bulk of a large rib rode the waves like a prize bull as it nosed round the cliff base, almost in the breaking surf which bounced off the rock. He spotted aboard four figures in dry suits. The rib was no more than twenty metres away now and just behind, to its port side, was the Great Stack, out of sight due to the overhanging rock. Jack felt a surge of adrenaline rush through his chilled body and his alarm bells spurred him to action. In a smooth movement, he dropped flipper first into a rising wave, at the same time sliding down his face mask. He was too late. A barrage of automatic fire ripped him apart as he disappeared beneath the swell and red spray like macabre graffiti splattered the vacated barnacle ledge.

Chapter 1

A Fennec helicopter skimmed low over the mountains of the Western Highlands. There was a heavy plastering of snow. Two-fit looking men in wind-proofs were climbing the West Ridge of Beinn a 'Glo and they turned into a biting north east wind at the sound of helicopter turbines echoing from somewhere below in Glen Uiske. Then they spotted it, 300 metres lower, emerging from a blanket of sleet. It was heading east over the rising ground with a bealach, or saddle, directly ahead. A snow flurry rolled towards it from the col with the fluidity of a powder avalanche, almost obliterating it as if covering it with a magician's white cloth.

"What the hell, David," the bigger of the two spat out, cupping a gloved hand to the side of his mouth. "That doesn't look good."

"You can say that again, Duncan," his friend shouted. "An accident about to happen; there are 200 metres of rock directly ahead of it."

Both men stepped back from the exposed icy edge which fell in a single sweep of Torridonian sandstone and verglas to the glen below. Though they listened intently there was no explosion or indication of sudden impact.

"They're bloody mad to be flying that low," Duncan muttered, more to himself than to his companion, taking off his mitts and brushing the hoar off the front pocket of his anorak. He continued, "I'll try and get a signal on my mobile, but there's not much hope in this hellhole of speaking to anybody; no wonder Glen Uiske was once known as the Devil's Arsehole."

"I think that was a misnomer of a white settler, Duncan who didn't have the Gaelic!" David gave a laugh which was snatched by a gust.

After trying various positions on the knife-edged ridge, Duncan gave a wave with a now gloved hand, indicating that they should move on.

"We'll try again as we head for the summit, Dave," he yelled. "At least we should get a signal from the top."

"Let's take this rope off," his friend suggested as he joined him, giving the coils a flick which launched a flurry of snow flakes. "It'll slow us up."

Duncan called, "I'm worried, for I doubt if even that old work horse, the Sea King, would venture into that corrie today and they'll fly into hell itself. Come to think of it, there would be no icing problems there. Good idea, lad," he added, "about the rope." He continued, unclipping, "I've a bad feeling about that helicopter."

"So you identified the chopper, Duncan?"

"Yes. I was in one at a Search and Rescue conference in the Bavarian Alps. But it doesn't fit." He knocked some balled up snow from his crampons with his ice axe. I knew that it was a Eurocopter right away: it's quite distinctive, one of the top high altitude choppers in the business. Some have rescued climbers at over 8000 metres." Deep in thought, he handed the rope end to his companion and continued. "It's also a nippy bugger, Dave, almost 287 kph and a range of 650 km without having a fresh swig of paraffin. Quite a machine, but what the hell is it doing here in a full blown blizzard?"

The difficulties on the ridge were greater than expected and belatedly they realised that it was stupid to climb unroped. Classified as Grade 4, the West Ridge was a serious route for top mountaineers in good winter conditions; the current conditions were not good. The verglas, like polished armour, encased the rock. On top was a treacherous covering of windswept powder. Verglas forms by sublimation – directly from a super cooled vapour to a solid. The points of their crampons protested, emitting a metallic rasping as chrome molly steel tried to get a grip such conditions can cause the points to snap off.

"Just the weather for a call-out, Dave," Duncan shouted into the wind. He continued shouting. "The sort of day when I would have cursed a casualty for being stupid to go out in the first place."

"Just think of adventure – like going for that fateful last crap," Dave shouted back, looking up. "Anyhow, let's get out of it."

"Adventure be damned." Duncan drew the back of a mitt across his brow to reveal a tanned, strong, lined face below the rime. It was a face empty of emotion no matter what nature threw at it: there was no arrogance, just a sense of power which emanated from the big man as if he were an offshoot of the mountain. He now paused after having scraped up a difficult ice-choked chimney with an elegance one would not have expected: a ballet on plastered rock. They had almost run out of mountain. The wind was petulant and emitted a sharp cracking noise like a whiplash. From time to time it produced a low deep whistle as if

congratulating itself. He shouted to Dave who was strug-
gling on the iced corner.

"Dave, the lee side of a rock just ahead might be sheltered
enough to try the mobile again."

As his friend emerged from the pitch, splattered with
fresh snow, Duncan pointed ahead with his ice axe. "If I
remember correctly the top is just ahead – it should be a
dawdle now."

As they went round to the back of the rock gendarme,
Dave spoke in more moderate tones. "Ah, this is better. What
a bloody gale!" He looked about furtively at the boiling
snow drifting below. "Nothing like a few thousand tons of
solid rock to act as a draught excluder, Duncan." He swung
his pack off and slipped out the coiled rope from the top
flap and placed it on a snow-covered boulder. "May as well
be comfortable as you try that infernal device."

Duncan took his mitts off and struggled to operate his
phone. His chunky fingers punched out an emergency number
and he gave a grimace of satisfaction as he heard the ringing
tone. Like a conjuror, David produced a stainless steel
thermos. Duncan gave a thumbs up.

"Hello, Margaret. This is Duncan MacGillvery, the
Mountain Rescue Team Leader.

"Do you think I'm hard of hearing, Duncan, though
with that roaring noise over the phone it sounds as if you
are in a wind tunnel."

"You're about right, Mags. We're on top of a mountain
in a storm. Can you put me through to the super? An emergency."

"Hold on." Her soft Hebridean accent had undertones
of quiet efficiency.

"What is it, Duncan?" It was the more sonorous voice
of Chief Superintendent John Montgomery.

"I'm on top of Beinn a'Glo, the peak at the head of Coire Uiske. I'm with David Bell, doc from Inverness, who's with the Team."

"Go on, I'm listening, but I can barely hear you."

"The weather's foul, John." As quickly as possible Duncan gave the facts of the mystery chopper.

"Right, Duncan. I'll make enquiries with Air Traffic Control, I'll try and contact you on the half hour and the hour."

"Thanks, John." Duncan took a gulp of black coffee... "Aye, David, you make a fine brew. I'm thinking we'd better get to hell down. We're in for a big fall of snow."

"I don't think we'll ever see that chopper again – even if it did come down, Duncan."

"If it ditched, I reckon it will be a job for the SAR choppers and their FLIR, the infra-red, though the distress beacon should activate."

"We'll go back home via the Coire Uiske col, anyhow, Dave. You never know ...." His voice trailed off as he moved into the full force of the gale.

"I assumed you were going to say that," his friend yelled back, tightening the draw cord on his anorak hook. Duncan led through the now knee-deep snow and, turning his head, he again addressed Dave.

"I think we had better keep a weather eye out for avalanches and it will take us at least an hour to descend to Bealach Uiske." Dave raised his ice axe in acknowledgement.

However, it was over an hour before they stumbled on the col. Visibility was almost zero and the snow was drifting badly. They floundered into a depression which gave some respite from the blast, then stopped and, brushing snow off his anorak, Duncan pulled out his mobile.

"It's strange that the Super hasn't called back, Duncan. Perhaps there's no signal?"

At that precise moment Duncan's mobile emitted the clarion tones of 'The Hen's March to the Midden', a popular Shetland tune, his idea of a joke.

"Duncan here."

"John Montgomery, Duncan. Can you hear me?"

"Yes, just, John – any news?"

"No, I've drawn a blank I have been trying to get you a couple of times," and he added, "there's no report of a missing aircraft or a Mayday – I checked with RAF Lossiemouth as well, but one of my constables who was at the shore of the wee Minch did hear an engine about fifteen minutes before you phoned. He couldn't see anything due to cloud and snow," he continued, "the engines sounded normal as far as he could tell. That's the only lead I've got and it was heading in the general direction of the co-ordinates you gave."

"Copied, John. We're at the Uiske Bealach now. Conditions are grim; we'll be heading east to the B391 single track road and will give a call if we come across anything."

"OK, Duncan. Give Dr Bell my regards."

Duncan had meantime sat down in the deep snow. He looked up at the plastered, Arctic figure of his companion in disbelief.

"I don't know if you heard that, Dave, but there's no report of a Mayday, though one of the bobbies on the west coast heard an aircraft heading our way about the right time."

"Did he have a visual?"

"Not really, the clag had moved in. The plot thickens," Duncan mused, "and I have a bad feeling in my bones and don't tell me it's osteoarthritis."

"Let's get to hell out of here before we have to tunnel," the doctor muttered. "I could do with getting my feet up –

and not in the bowels of some avalanche! Don't act the hypochondriac, that's the nine to five part of my job! You've never had an illness in your life."

Walking in line a short distance apart, the two ghostly figures made their way across the now relatively flat area of the col. Their compasses, which hung round their necks, were checked from time to time in the gloom and every so often Duncan would verify their exact position with his GPS. Though they didn't mention it, they realised that it would be at least one and half hours back to Dave's car and that they would have to call on all their reserves to get through the drifts – or even could be forced to dig a snow hole.

It was about the third occasion that Duncan took a GPS reading. He was again ahead of Dave, when the doctor thought he heard a dull metallic rasping noise at his right foot. Plunging a snow-plastered mitt into the foothold, he immediately came across a circular object which he inspected in the beam of his headlamp which they were now using. At first he thought it was an old metal cap for some container and was about to throw it back into the snow but, pausing for an instant, he stuffed it into his anorak pocket. He thought this irrational: collecting scrap metal when the purpose was to get out of this hell-hole alive. When he re-started the plod-plod treadmill behind Duncan, he speculated on the symptoms of hypothermia, a subject into which he had done some research. In fact, irrational behaviour was one of its symptoms, such as throwing away essentials like ruck-sack or gloves and even imagining that stream water was running uphill.

Scotland has a well deserved reputation for violent weather, being in the path of Atlantic storms. The cold, damp conditions can act like a wick, sucking life-preserving heat from the body. But he dismissed hypothermic thoughts;

he knew it was because he was tired and probably was already suffering mild exposure. Ten minutes later the curtain of snow turned to a speckled darkness, exploding in a brilliant spasm of white and he saw Duncan's phantasmagoric frame silhouetted against the light. The explosion would have made a great promo for the Apocalypse. In a millisecond the shock wave hit him, flattening him backwards into the snow, burying him in a cold white sheet.

Chapter 2

A tall, lithe girl wearing a short azure blue skirt and an expensive white silk top sat down at a table shaded by a large umbrella on the café terrace. The umbrella had a bright floral pattern which caught the slanting beams. She swivelled her sun glasses up on her blonde hair and scanned the menu. There were inquisitive and appreciative glances from the few early customers. Close by, a swarthy man with a ski jump nose ordered a three shot latte to usher him into the new day. But the blonde girl had no interest in him. A crisp waiter with a white towel over his left forearm as if about to negotiate a surrender sidled to her table. En route he fussily adjusted a chair which had strayed out of line.

"Mademoiselle?"

"Cappucino, garcon."

"The usual?"

"Merci."

The winter sun still had warmth and here in La Rochelle, where in the tenth century a fishing village once stood, the scene was serene. The locals insist that La Rochelle has the finest climate in all France and they're probably right.

Michelle Scott gave a gleaming smile to the waiter when he returned after having shattered the relative quiet with the coffee machine. Tentatively dipping her long spoon into froth, she looked absorbed.

Just then there was the distinctive note of a supercharged Mercedes, less abrasive than the racket of a Rapid Express. The car glided to the kerb and a fit, tall figure stepped out holding an attaché case. Two tanned youths stopped in admiration, obviously excited, and spoke in English.

"Six hundred and fifty horse power?" one quizzed

The tall driver smiled and replied, "I see you know your Grande Tourers."

The smaller of the two gave a low whistle and shook his head. "Magnifique."

Michelle stood up and waved. She was animated at the arrival of her fiancé, Derek Hawthorne. "I'm here."

He looked round and raised a hand. She watched as he strode up to her table. His face was weather beaten and clean shaven. A scar, a paler shade of brown, extended from his lower right ear along the line of his chin for a full seven centimetres, a memento from Oman. If anything, it enhanced the line of his jaw. He swung his briefcase on to the table and stooped down to give her a kiss.

"How's my pet archaeologist? Dug up anything interesting?"

"Not since I saw you last. Have you had any luck?" she quizzed as he sat down.

"Well, not really." He casually looked round the adjoining tables and lightly rubbed the side of his nose with his forefinger.

"Coffee, Derek?"

"Sure." He raised a hand to the waiter who was giving the now fortified nosey man his change.

"Can't be too careful, girl. Lots of people snooping about with big ears as well as big noses."

"I got your proboscis message."

"It's no bigger than other parts of my anatomy." He gave her a broad grin just as his coffee arrived.

"Size isn't everything," she returned demurely, taking another sip of her coffee and looking seductively over the foam which she had just beheaded.

"I may have found something, Michelle."

"Oh?" She arched her dark brows.

"Have a look at this." He took a mobile phone from his pocket and punched up an image then passed it to her. She angled it on the table and studied the screen intently. "It appears like a stool with several legs." She turned her gaze towards him. The sun was turning Derek's hair a light copper colour and a Jackdaw landed on their table and cocked his head as if he, too, was puzzled, more likely because there was nothing to eat.

"That's a good guess," he said. "When we enlarge it, you'll realise your stool is a rock, with its chunky legs in the drink, possibly the sea depicted by minutely carved waves as you can see. Let me elaborate."

"Go on," she encouraged. "I'm all ears – no anatomical pun intended."

"As you know, I've been looking here for clues in several ancient ruins for evidence of the alleged Crusader hoard in the Templars' fleet of ships." She nodded. He continued. "You told me of the eighteen ships which put in here, in La Rochelle, on October 12th 1307."

"That's not gospel," Michelle returned thoughtfully "Shall we say that could be historical speculation." She carried on, turning her attention once more to the photo. "From the image, it looks like a wood carving?"

"That's right, possibly ship's timber. I found it under rubble at the old monastery in the next valley over. I went just before dawn."

"Oh, I heard you sneaking out, but I'm well trained – I didn't let on."

He ignored this and continued. "It's possibly an oak fragment from a ship's frame. Could you carbon date it or SE Dendrochronology?"

"What size?"

"About the area of the menu."

"Condition?"

"Pretty good, I would say; seems solid. It was buried underneath a flat piece of limestone. In fact, I only came across it when I lifted the slab up as I was distracted by a super green lizard which I thought had scuttled underneath and I wanted a closer look at it – the lizard, I mean."

"Have you got it with you?"

"No, it's at the flat. I put it away; somehow or other I think it's important."

"Umph," she murmured. "Damn it, man, you've got me turned on. You know that I can't resist academic temptations."

"Oh, another thing," he smiled. "Though it's difficult to see on that small screen, there's a minute cross carved in the background."

"And," there was now excitement showing in Michelle's deep blue eyes – "and," she repeated, "you're stringing me along, you bastard. Give."

"It's a Knights Templar cross, I'm pretty sure of it," he returned.

"I see what you mean" she said in a low voice. "If the specimen is suitable, I may be able to have it dated under my research programme back at Cambridge."

"Fantastic. I know I had odds stacked against me to find

any clue at all here; I came to get the atmosphere. It just shows you; one never knows."

"By the way, when I searched the maritime records in Seville, Derek, I came across a reference on speculation as to where the Templar goodies may have gone."

"Oh, you didn't mention this."

"I did, but I put it down to historians' fancy. You probably don't remember; it's complicated and you know most of it already. After all, you're the one who thought of a follow up on the Crusades after your five year stint in booby trapped badlands and," she added as an afterthought, "a suitable recuperation hobby."

"Is my history lesson finished, miss?"

"Not quite, and pay attention ... let me make it simple for you. You don't appreciate the romance of history. I'll condense it." She smiled widely. "Listen this time..."

"Go on."

"Well, the Grand Master of the Knights Templar, Jacques de Molay, and his two side kicks were accused of heresy by the papal commission. It was a frame–up by King Phillip IV of France who had the pope in his waistcoat pocket. Also, he owed the Templars a great deal, of money. His vast debt was matched by a proportional hatred and envy of the wealth of the Order. The Grand Master renounced a trumped up heresy confession publicly, together with Geoffrey de Charney, and they were then promptly arrested by the French as 'relapsed heretics'. Both men were burned at the stake and Jacques de Molay uttered a curse which became legendary and known as the Curse of the Templars. 'Within one year God will summon both Clement and Phillip to His Judgement."

"Michelle," Derek interrupted. "It's been about six months since I got hooked on the Crusades. That was when

I first mentioned it, but I was already interested when I was in the services."

"That's right." She gave him another broad smile, her teeth catching the sun beams which were darting between fronds of a resident palm. "Yes, a new life lay ahead when you got out but, as I indicated, it was boring. I can suggest something else, Colonel Hawthorne." She playfully wagged a long finger at him. "You could always buy a Crusader War Game... at least your life expectancy would be higher than in your old job."

"I knew that you'd think me senile, taking an interest in medieval history." Derek ran his fingers through his hair. "That's the trouble with the scientific brain: you have to have facts, artefacts, bits of bone and bloody rusted cannon balls, though I must admit I thought I had aroused your feline curiosity."

"You know damned well you have, you oaf. That's what grabbed me about my job – trying to re-assemble seized up jigsaw events of hundreds or even thousands of years ago. Only," she went on, "don't think that I'm not interested in clues – that's my job, tedious as it may be."

Michelle paused for an instant, then looked at him intently. "About this time, Derek, Robert the Bruce was laying waste his enemies in Scotland. In reality he was a frog, a Frenchman, as you know, and as a warrior king had many of the Crusaders' aspirations. Scotland would be an obvious sanctuary for the treasure ships. Also, many Scottish families had sons, knights, who went on the Crusades; the ships could disappear in the labyrinth of Scotland's west coast.

"I like that, Michelle. For a scientist you make a good speculator." He gave a deep laugh which now made the scar on his face look alive, like a duplicate smile. He laid a large hand on her shoulder and stood up.

"Come on, my girl. Let's go back to the flat and see if I can further foster your interest in my piece of wood."

"Now you're talking soldier."

The flat was in an old part of town, but it was modernised and snuggled away in a quiet cul de sac.

"Have you had breakfast, Derek?" She was standing at the arch leading into the small kitchen. Her hand was raised in an enquiring gesture. It was a simple action, with a forefinger raised as if addressing a favourite pupil.

"How about you getting a look at the firewood first?'

"I'm all for that."

Derek went to the window and, taking a casual look out, opened it. From behind a potted plant on the footprint veranda he withdrew a long sock and took it over to the breakfast bar, then carefully slid a small section of timber on to the tiled top. Michelle sidled over and, putting a hand affectionately on Derek's knee, looked down at the object with interest. She then slid on to a bar stool and picked up the nondescript piece of wood with reverence. Her trained eye at a glance had already assimilated various salient points and possibilities. "I may be able to get a core from it, Derek." She added "and it feels reasonably solid. It must be hardwood of some description, but I will be able to discover that in the lab; we have masses of info relating to 'archaeological ships' timbers on file."

"And the several legged stool?"

"I'm still sitting on that one." She gave a long pause. "Fascinating. Can you fetch my laptop, Derek? It's under the bed in my spare rucksack," she continued abstractly. "I may be able to get a better look at it. I have a macro lens for my Nikon with me as well as a microscopic facility for the computer. We should get a reasonable image and I've got the extra programme for enhancing."

"Great," the big man enthused. "I'll rustle up an omelette or something while you do your stuff. Some say good old digital, others think it's the building block of destruction."

It was some forty minutes later that Derek placed a tray on the now cluttered breakfast bar.

"Grub's up," he announced as he made room for their brunch.

"I could do with some sustenance," Michelle returned. "My brain had switched to stools and crosses."

"Any progress?" he asked as he poured out two mugs of coffee.

"Have a look at this." She swivelled the laptop round to reveal a high resolution image of the wood carving. "I'm quite pleased with it; the filters made an incredible difference."

"Phew." He gave a half whistle. "That's cool. You're a clever girl."

"My vote is for good old digital," she smiled, picking up a finger of fresh toast.

Derek was still holding a forkful of mushroom omelette, poised in midair. He put it down on his plate without touching it. "Quite remarkable," he muttered. "What do you think? What do you think Michelle?" he repeated.

Her scientific training switched her into conservative mode. "It looks a genuinely old carving," she admitted. "And the cross is intriguing. It depicts the original Crusaders' Cross, which is a complicated design. There were several Crusader crosses, but this," she pointed with her knife, "is an early cross which shows a commitment, a pledge to fight, and differs from the cross of the Hospitaller Order, for example, which is really a Greek cross and that eventually developed into the Maltese cross. However," she continued, now tucking into the food, "it's all very vague and specialised and I'll have to confer with my terra firma colleagues to get more info."

Derek once more raised his fork. But it did not stop him speaking. "The stool or possible fort is curious. It could be a squat rock tower on those stumpy legs, even a fort, and apparently in the sea."

"That's right," she ruminated, "and the carved cross has been specifically planted on it, as if it was a nameplate. Very curious, or perhaps," she ventured, "to give it some clout – some validity."

"I know what you mean and it's more apparent now that it's been enlarged. What about the wood?" he asked.

"Your guess is as good as mine. I doubt now if it was part of the ship's frame or structure, but carbon dating or some of the new software programmes may give a further lead."

"A piece of furniture?" he queried, demolishing the remains of his meal. "Ornamental carving or suchlike?"

"Not fine enough for that. This is," she glanced at the screen again, "rustic; as if it was an illustration, perhaps, symbolic as on a map – conveying something..." her voice trailed off. "Though it's artistically executed," she speculated, speaking slowly, "yet it seems hurriedly done as if not meant for ornamentation."

"Shall we head back to the UK," he questioned her, "to try and get the carbon dating done?"

"Suits me," she answered, "and possibly some other tests. As mentioned, I have work to do at the university and I must say that I'm intrigued with your find. Not necessarily that I think that here lies some lead to long lost loot," she nodded towards the rather nondescript piece of wood on the tiles, "but perhaps some further clue pertaining to Knights Templar history."

"While you beaver away in the lab I think I'll pay a visit to some of my Scottish friends. "I'll drop you off at the uni and you can come up and join me in haggis country. I've always promised to show you round the real Scotland."

"You know that I love Scotland," she replied eagerly. "Let's pack."

Chapter 3

It was as if the blizzard had been stopped in its tracks by the violence of the explosion. There appeared to be a momentary truce with the elements. The wind had eased, but when David gathered his thoughts and his headlamp, then struggled out of the drift, he realised that it was probably the insulation of the snow in which he was partly buried that had caused the illusion. Fine powder had penetrated his windproof suit via the gap at the side of his anorak hood and was now melting on his thermal vest. He shook himself and pondered for a few seconds, then gently rubbed his smarting eyes with the fine powder snow. This gave immediate relief. His next thought was how the hell could his headlamp have come off? It had been attached by its headband round his helmet, which in turn had been enclosed by his hood and this was still pulled tight and locked by its cord toggle. Then he recalled that people blown up in explosions had literally come out of their shoes, which had remained where they were.

"Duncan," he shouted. "Duncan."

Now he realised what had happened, or at least recalled

the violent explosion and seeing the macabre image of his friend. It had been like a scene from no man's land.

Other than the dancing beam of his headlamp there was nothing visible but speeding, horizontal curtains of snow flakes. He was grateful that his compass still hung from its cord round his neck inside his anorak and he took it out, brushing it with a gloved hand, then he continued on his old bearing. It was imperative that he should find Duncan as soon as possible and wondered if he had been killed.

John Montgomery had not attained the rank of Chief Super-intendent at the age of forty-five by being a slouch. Indeed, he was precisely the opposite and was still an active hill runner. The day, so far, since the start of his shift, had been strange: a missing prawn fisherman somewhere in Loch Sweep with the coastguard chopper grounded due to bad visibility and that strange call from Duncan. He had an uneasy feeling about that and knew that the rescue Co-ordination Centre had also had concern when he was speaking with them. On impulse, he picked up the phone, for he hadn't heard from Dr Bell or Duncan for several hours and the shipping forecast, which he always listened to, predicted Violent Storm 11 for the area just west of where they were. John was descended from a long line of fishermen, at least four of whom had been lost at sea. The upper echelon of wind speeds in the shipping forecast always gave him a feeling of foreboding. That chap, Sir Francis Beaufort who originally classified them did a good job, but that was for the sea; add a few hundred or thousand metres on to this for altitude and Force 11 (at 103 km), plus the wind chill factor, and the shit hits the proverbial fan. You don't have to have a wild imagination to visualise such conditions. However, he still had a greater fear of the sea. Thoughts on his lineage were interrupted...

Sergeant Alec MacDougal's, crisp, clipped, efficient voice had answered the call.

"John Montgomery here, Alec."

"Oh, hello, sir. What can I do for you?"

The Superintendent outlined the facts of the aircraft and his concern that the two climbers hadn't called in.

"What do you suggest, sir?"

"I don't think that we should pull out all the stops just yet, Alec, but can you go up the B931 road and see if you can find the doc's car? You'll get the details of it from Traffic. I think it will be about twenty miles up, after a wee hump-backed bridge. If you look at the map, you may get a better idea. It was parked there for their return from the head of Coire Uiske Bealach; as I mentioned, they were climbing Beinn a'Glo. To tell you the truth, I don't know what the hell we can do with the forecast as it is." He added, "Probably it's just that their mobile battery has run out of steam. Oh, by the way, Duncan's number is on the call-out list. Keep me informed at home, Alec, and ask the team to stand by just in case."

"Wilco."

Just as the Superintendent was about to leave his office, with his cap and anorak on, the snow started to fall, sticking to the window. He paused for a second and went to his desk and rang Duncan's number again. It was still unobtainable. He put the phone down thoughtfully and made a mental note to get in touch with Duncan's mobile provider. They may be able to do a trace.

Dr David Bell gathered his thoughts. He realised that he was suffering from shock and was feeling the biting cold. He tried to be methodical. Fortunately, he hadn't lost any of his gear and, wiping snow from his face and the edge of his anorak hood, he started to move forward. There was no sign of Duncan's prints and a white darkness was pressing down. He checked his bearing and knew that he would get to where he had last seen his friend in minutes.

A Gaelic oath was the first indication that Duncan was alive and, sweeping the surface with the head of his ice axe, David cleared the ground powder which resembled a foam-covered sea. He inched his way forward knee deep and called.

"Duncan, Duncan?" Then there was a muffled, angry shout "Get off my bloody face, you idiot.

"You're standing on me..."

"Sorry, man," David responded, "didn't know that you were buried."

In a few minutes the doctor had cleared the powder off his companion; it was as light as polystyrene. He saw that Duncan's face was a mass of blood. The apparition spoke: "Good God, man, what hit me? Is it still night?"

"Can you see my headlamp, Duncan?"

"Just a faint glow, doc."

"I'll try and remove the blood from your eye sockets, it may help. Can you move your legs?"

"Let me try."

Duncan gingerly bent his knees, causing powder to cascade down like icing sugar, then moved both arms, easing himself up on his elbows."

"Yes, I'm still functioning, but I don't think I'll be entering the A'Chailleach Hill Race this Easter."

David observed Duncan's responses with relief, but he was still concerned with the big man's eyes.

"Let me get at you and see what I can do. It's a pity Halloween's past; you would have been a sensation."

"Very apt. What the hell was it – an explosion?"

"Oh, it was that all right, and a big one, more like a

bomb detonating." David piled snow behind his friend to act as a back rest and noted that his patient was able to raise himself into a sitting position. "More comfortable?"

"Yes, but can you turn that darned wind down?"

The doctor now shone the full beam of his headlamp directly on to Duncan's face again, but he didn't flinch. 'I'm going to use a treatment provided by mother nature, Duncan." He studied his patient's face carefully. As well as the eye trauma, there were a number of fine splinter wounds and burns, the first being the source of the bleeding. He continued. "This powder is what wind slab is formed from, with all the points of the snow crystals rubbed off in wind drift. It's ideal for clearing congealed blood and also acts as an anaesthetic. Can you see my light, now?" he questioned, gently removing the gory mess.

"Just the suspicion of a glow, Dave, but I think your DIY painkiller's working. I feel numb."

"My fingers agree with that hypothesis," David responded, then endeavoured to blow circulation back into his hands. "Have you still got the mobile?"

"It's in my anorak pouch."

David plunged a freezing hand into the pocket. The zip was in tatters and the pocket filled with snow. "Not any more."

"I guess it's not our day." Duncan slurred his words.

It took the doctor a further fifteen minutes to clean his friend's face and remove most of the blood. He could now see the facial injuries. Apart from a deep gash on his right cheek, the loss of his eyelashes and eyebrows, the damage was less than he expected. The eyes were bloodshot, but it was impossible to ascertain tissue damage.

"There's a mouthful of coffee left in my flask. Do you think that you could swallow some?"

"I could have a go." Duncan tried to sound enthusiastic.

David slid off his rucksack and found the thermos among snow debris which had got inside, despite the tightened draw cord. He poured the best part of a cupful of the still hot liquid and handed it to his friend.

"Drink slowly, in sips. Your throat may be scalded."

"It tastes like a phosphorous cocktail," Duncan spluttered, "but it's great."

"We have to make a decision, Duncan. We can either bivvy here or try and get lower, out of this bloody wind. It's up to you."

"You know as well as me, Dave, we should move down. Let's use a short length of rope and you can have me on a lead. If you keep the rope under tension you will be able to feel if I'm OK. If I remember correctly, the descent to the bealach is not too difficult and there are some monster boulders down there if we want to stop for bed without breakfast." He took another mouthful of coffee. "We have to get out of the hell-hole, Dave. There's no decent place up here to excavate a snow hole and if we dig a hole straight down and sit in it, even in our bivvy bags, we could suffocate with all this powder.

"My exact thoughts, but I'll have a root about to see if I can unearth your mobile. Any ideas?"

"No, none. I felt as if I was airborne at one stage with the explosion."

"Well, that puts paid to that. By the way, have you any idea what caused the big bang, Duncan, the explosion?" He was taking snow goggles out of his rucksack and he put them on Duncan. "These may give you some protection, though it's a bit late."

"Thanks," Duncan replied, adjusting them with difficulty, and stood up as if expecting to keel over, but he revived.

"I'm not sure what happened I didn't have time to think, yet at the same time it seemed in slow motion, though I had time to deduce that I was going more up than down initially, which I knew was wrong in the greater scheme of things, for my final destination was emphatically downwards."

"At least for a blind man you still have a sense of humour."

Sergeant Alec MacDougall rang the Deputy Leader, Wallace Dalgleish, of the Glen Dubh Mountain Rescue Team and told him of the Superintendent's concern.

"There's probably nothing to it, Wallace. He was using his mobile and it ran out of juice. But I'm going up with a couple of the Team to Dr David's car to check things out."

There was a pause, then Wallace, who always erred on the side of caution, replied. "OK, Alec, I'll follow with an advance party and take the coms wagon. It will perhaps save time later, though," he added, "I can't imagine anything that Duncan and Dave couldn't handle with their combined experience."

"We'll see you up at Dave's car, then."

"Right."

Superintendent John Montgomery had a good meal provided by his longsuffering wife, Elizabeth. He still had some ten years left before retirement, but was already having ideas of what he would do with his free time and reflected quite often on how much easier it would be to spend his leisure on the pension of Deputy Chief Constable or, dare he think it, even Chief.

"I enjoyed that, Liz," he congratulated his wife. "Nothing like tatties and mince to put lead in your pencil. It's the next best thing since tatties and herring your piñatas skatin."

"Och, awa wi yer havering," she retorted. "You and the guid old days. What about the reek from the lum and digging peats for ten hours so that you could shiver by the fire all winter."

"Where's your romance, woman,..." He gave a bellow of a laugh. "You go and slave over those dirty dishes and relish auld lang syne."

As he retreated to his office he heard a muffled oath which he was sure would have been disapproved of by the Wee Free Kirk. John had a quirky habit which concerned the toilet. Though never tight with money, he had a hang–up when it came to toilet rolls. He hated using them and their soft unpredictability or the slick, cheaper brands with a low coefficient of friction. Both he found spooky. This phobia could be sourced to the finite length of the rolled cylinder. Its life span seemed symbolic – like Eliot's coffee spoons. How many days were left: when will it end? His family had been poor, especially if the fishing was bad when he was raised in Durness. This was a small fishing village whose compact, neat cottages were built at the edge of the machair. Ironically, these buildings had originated as black houses, so called due to lack of both light and ventilation for peat smoke. It was a tranquil place, when there wasn't a storm and the margin of golden sand contrasted vividly with a turquoise sea. Often the wind blew from Arctic Norway, which painted a white edge to breakers, patrolled by mocking gulls. In the spring the machair, the wonderful grass of these latitudes, provided a verdant backcloth with a riot of wild flowers, creating a confetti-like bed cover. There were random stacks of photogenic creels and the odd upturned boat displaying its private parts. Then, of course, there were the nomadic black-faced sheep which appeared on speaking terms with the locals who knew each by name.

He wasn't exactly sure when he found a remedy to his unfortunate affliction. It probably came when he was a young boy still at primary school in the form of a folded copy of the *North Eastern Gazette*, which had been jammed between the cistern pipe and the wall of the toilet. Perhaps his sister or brother had been caught short, or his mum may have put it there for an emergency. Ever since he had a copy of a newspaper with him when he went about his daily business. He also discovered that even an out-of-date broadsheet or tabloid had the added advantage of some snippet of news which helped to pass the time. No one had ever commented on the fact that he regularly had the same paper with him for several days and that it became progressively thinner as the week advanced. It was a point of principle with him that on the last day in his current paper's active life (give or take stomach upsets or constipation) he used the obituary page as a farewell gesture. Even he thought this strange, but it appealed to his sense of humour.

John picked up the phone and asked headquarters to put him through to Duncan's mobile provider. This way he felt he would have more clout as in the past there had been a certain reluctance by the company to give full co-operation with police enquiries. However, there must have been a change of staff for their new head of department couldn't have been more co-operative.

"I will put our engineers on to it right away, Superintendent, and come back ASAP." John gave him his home number and hung up.

Meantime, the two climbers were in dire straits. After Duncan had fallen for the fourth time, they realised the short guide rope was not working. Both were covered in white hoar and Duncan was staggering, due either to sheer exhaustion or to the fact that he couldn't see.

"Let's take this bloody rope off, Duncan. It's a case of

the blind leading the blind." There was a trace of exasperation and almost fear in the doctor's voice.

"Are we down at the big boulders yet, Dave?" Duncan's voice was weak and was decimated by the wind.

"I think we are. It's difficult to tell: snow, snow and more snow. You will have gathered that the slope has eased so I think we may be in the North Corrie. Also, there are what appear to be white sugar cubes about three metres high dotted about which may be boulders in drag, but at the moment I can only see the length of a decent spit – you're not missing much."

"These will be the big erratics, the size of furniture vans not sugar lumps. Some, the ones with cavities beneath, were used way back by crofters as summer sheilings, when they took the black cattle up for the fresh grass. We might find at least a cranny in which to shelter. If we don't, I think that there will be two new frozen erratics come morning."

"Good idea, Duncan. I'll coil the rope and give you a shoulder to lean on. I don't want you to fall down a hole."

They made their way through the drifts and skirted one huge snow-covered rock which was overhanging on the lee side. In minutes, they broke through a deep drift which was abutting the rock face and stumbled into a sheltered area between the overhanging rock and the snow. It was like heaven, with the thermostat turned down.

"Sit down, Duncan, our luck's changed."

The big man collapsed with his hands outspread behind him and leaned against the rock. "Just what the doctor ordered," he muttered.

"I'll get the wee Gaz stove out, Duncan, and, would you believe it, we may even manage a brew."

"I thought when you suggested taking bivvy gear and the stove that it was a bit of overkill, Dave. Other than on a rescue I've never had to spend a night out on a Scottish mountain. I now sit corrected and it could be a life saver," he added with a grimace. "I can't wait to get into my bivvy bag."

Dave shone a tired headlamp beam on his companion's face again. He was taken aback. The snow goggles which he had put on Duncan were encased in ice with a reddish tinge. His face was blanked over as if plastered smooth with a distorted hole where his mouth was hidden.

"Good God, man," the doctor spluttered, "you look like the Hulk!"

"I feel like him," was the instant reply. "What about that brew?"

"MacGillvery, you are incorrigible."

Chapter 4

John Montgomery didn't sleep well and when the phone rang at 3.10 am he felt a surge of relief. Elizabeth turned over with a sigh and muttered something about being too old to have night calls. The Superintendent picked up the mobile which was on the bedside table and swung his long legs on to the floor. As he strode out on to the landing, he spoke quietly. "John Montgomery."

"This is Ivor Smith, Alba Communications. Sorry that I'm so late in getting back to you, Superintendent, but some of our masts were damaged in the storm and we had a lot of trouble cross checking."

"Any luck?" the policeman barked, immediately regretting the impatience in his voice, and walked into the lounge. The remnants of the coal fire were still glowing.

"Yes, from our records we managed to plot a position before the mobile went dead. The final signal was weak and intermittent; in fact it was just transmission tone, no speech," he continued. "We have made a copy of your earlier conversations with... a Duncan somebody?"

"MacGilivery," John prompted.

"That's it. The cross bearings for the two previous calls which you had with MacGillvery were very close geographically. The second was relayed from a different mast, Storr on the Isle of Skye, which means the subscriber, MacGilivery, had moved only a short distance north east in the intervening time." He paused. "If you want to take down the GPS co-ordinates, I'll give them to you now."

"Shoot, Ivor, I have a pen." There was a pause as John scribbled down the numbers. "Got that, many thanks. If you can send a hard copy to police headquarters, I'll get it in the morning. Also a record of the conversations. I'll arrange any necessary clearance."

"Glad to be of help, Superintendent. I'll do that. Goodnight."

John then went out to the hall and picked up his two-way radio which he had left on the charger, then returned to the lounge where he put some kindling on the remains of the fire. Soon, fingers of reflected warm light were dancing on the floral wallpaper. He switched to the Mountain Rescue frequency.

"Glendhu Rescue Base, come in please, John Montgomery speaking: Over."

Almost immediately there was a reply. "Sergeant MacDougall, pass your message."

"Anything to report, Sergeant?"

"Negative. We're parked alongside Dr Bell's car, but there's no sign of them. Conditions are crap, but Wallace Daigleish and half a dozen of the Team are headed up towards the Bealach Uiske, though I doubt if they'll make it."

"I can understand that. Perhaps you can relay to them, or they may even have picked this up. I had a check from the mobile company on Duncan's last phone transmission, but there was no audio, just a transmit tone and that has

been pinpointed at just your side of the bealach. Wallace –
if you read this, it looks as if they were heading back to the
car, but it's a long way, as you know."

"Glen Dubh hill party calling John Montgomery. Wallace
here, got your message to Base. Come in: Over."

"Go ahead, Wallace."

"We will have to return, conditions too severe."

"Got that, you had better stand down till first light: Over."

"Did you also get that, Sergeant? Over"

"Affirmative, we will leave someone here in the event
that Duncan and Dr Bell make it."

"Fine, Sergeant. Set up the usual procedures."

"Wilco, goodnight."

Before heading home from police headquarters,
Sergeant Alec MacDougall as Duty Sergeant contacted
Roads. The reason for this was that when Wallace and the
Team returned from their abortive mission the snow had
completely covered the doctor's car. This and the fact that
the police 4 x 4 had problems getting back to Glen Dubh.
They told him that a rotary plough would be out within the
hour. An SAR chopper was also requested to standby. He
felt that the two climbers would get back on their own,
since logical procedure for them, given the severity of the
storm, was to bivouac. His final call was to alert SARDA,
the Search and Rescue Dog Association.

So far north, dawn is a non-event in winter, especially
when the weather is foul. Ghostly darkness transforms the
uniform wet blanket to a whitish grey and it can stay like
that all day. However, as the column of 4 x 4 vehicles made
its way up the snow channel that was the B391, they noted
that the clinical sculpture of the white trench stood as
testimony to the council's tenacity.

"Willie Hay." It was Sergeant Alec MacDougall speaking.

"Would you stop that bloody dog of yours slavering down my neck, it smells as if it's been feeding on braxy."

"What's braxy, Alec?"

"Carrion to you, Willie. What your ancestors lived on."

"You know, Sarge, Sgurr gets excited when there's a call-out. He either wants you to go faster or to get a good bite of MacGillvery," and added, "seeing carrion is scarce."

Dawn arrived with reluctance. Now, at least, the snow decided to fall vertically and slowly as if marking time. The cold was penetrating, assisted by the high humidity which ensured that it gained access to every cranny underneath the layers of pile clothing and breathable fabric.

The ten metre high pneumatic aerial was rising alongside the mountain rescue base truck when they arrived and some of the Team were already crammed inside or under the side awning which extended the length of the vehicle. The weather had abated overnight and the last of the vehicles slithered and parked in some sort of order. Dr Bell's car was isolated in the centre on the level patch of snow which resembled a white moat. Wallace turned as he entered the truck. The Sergeant was close behind.

"The road crew's made a sizeable clearance for us, Alec. Did you promise them a half bottle?"

"That could be termed bribery, but I must admit that this little arena is almost artistic."

Within a few minutes all the search party were gathered. Inside, a large LCD screen occupied the rear of the van.

When Wallace pushed his way in he put his laptop on a desk beneath an array of small monitors and the base station radio. He looked up and raised his voice which had a distinct Fife accent, difficult for strangers to decipher.

"OK, lads, let's have quiet." He switched the computer on and paused for a second. The wide screen came to life with boxes round the edges listing the various search groups, with grids marked clearly. It depicted a large map of the Bealach Uiske region. Immediately, there was quiet, just the static of the base set and an annoyed yelp from Sgurr as someone stood on his paw. Everyone realised this call-out was special. It was as if a cold hand had pressed down on every individual. The light from the fluorescent tubes on the ceiling spread an eerie funereal pallor on the faces.

"I presume you all know why we are here," Wallace commenced. "To search for Duncan and Dave ASAP. So let's get down to it." He paused once more. "First, Willie Hay and your dog together with two members, John and Cliff," he pointed at two climbers, "will head off immediately and search the area working up to the last lot of co-ordinates which are on the screen. You'll need GPS and also the hand mobile phone detector, but that could be a lost cause as I presume Duncan's mobile battery will be as flat as the Laraig Moor by this time."

"Right," Willie-the-dog, as he was known, responded.

"Incidentally" Wallace returned, addressing the rest of the Team, "if the weather improves we can expect a SAR chopper and also two RAF MR teams, should they be required, also back-up of more search dogs has been promised. Any update on the chopper, Sarge?"

"It's on standby, as you said, Wallace. We have to advise on conditions and vis."

"Good," the Deputy replied as he pressed the keyboard. A full size aerial photograph appeared. "Spent part of the night downloading this," he admitted, "But it gives a better idea of the place. There are a lot of boulders as you can see which could provide shelter but don't neglect the other search areas; they could be anywhere due to that storm."

"Is that cross on the photo the same as was on the map – where you reached last night?" It was the Sergeant speaking.

"That's right, Alec, not very far, is it? But it was desperate. The forecast's still poor, though better than yesterday and the wind's veering north west, force 5, poor visibility. Temperature -8c at a thousand metres. Avalanche risk Category 5. Put your avalanche transceivers on when you leave Base." He looked about, his thin face showing the strain; last night's fight in the blizzard, followed by hours compiling logistics had taken its toll. "Any questions?"

"Will our group following the dog party take a stretcher?" It was Donnie, local gamekeeper and a team member.

"Good idea. It will be central to the search area."

"I have a further point." Sergeant Alec stood up and looked round at the thirty or so Team members and some of his police colleagues. He cleared his throat for he had a lingering flu infection. "The Super asked me to outline the conversation he had with Duncan on his mobile yesterday when he was on the climb." He then gave a full account of John Montgomery's exchange with Duncan and last co-ordinates from the mobile provider. "You see the two positions of the separate calls at the bottom of the screen. This information should be kept confidential as there may be a logical explanation for the mystery helicopter – it's our two companions whom we are looking for today."

Chapter 5

"How are you, Duncan?" Dr David Bell's voice sounded muffled and distant.

"I've been worse, doc, but I can't remember when."

David switched on a tired headlamp and peered at his watch. "Good God, Duncan, it's 8 am."

"I think you've contracted a cold, David."

"So did I, but it's drifting snow. It's like a candy floss fairyland."

"I hope that after life is not going to be as cold as this," Duncan murmured, brushing snow and a small icicle off his balaclava. He had used his helmet as an uncomfortable seat overnight, then he thought for a moment. "You know, David, I think I've stumbled on a new form of torture. It could be called the 'commode treatment'. I thought I was in that final celestial white tunnel that looks a bigger version of one of those flexible drainage pipes. But I might have known that it wasn't leading to my destiny. It was probably just the glow of your torch."

"So you can see?"

"I'm not sure about that, but your torch is brighter than it was last night, and that doesn't add up."

"Thank goodness," the doctor murmured.

An hour later the staccato chop-chop of large rotors biting the air was heard at Base.

Sergeant MacDougall was stirring a cup of coffee. He had received a call from 377 Lima, the Merlin, a short time before giving their ETA. The Met at Squadron HQ had predicted a brief weather window. The big machine had all the electronic gismos of modern SAR. It inched its way above the tracks which started as a single trench, then divided after about four kilometres, heading for higher ground. Several of the Team of Grid B search area to the north had skis and made better progress in the deep powder despite the poor visibility. Within an hour they angled down to Coire Uiske Bealach. They relayed this information back to Base. Squadron Leader Simpson had an idea. He switched to the military frequency and called the Station's met officer. "This is the Captain 377 calling. We are now hoping to land at the rescue base due to poor visibility."

"Met here. How can I help?" He recognised the cultured tones of a new female officer which his crew had remarked upon, giving her 9 in a 1-10 classification.

"I was just checking our weather chart and as there seems to be a possibility of better weather to the south, I was wondering if there could be a chance of reaching our search co-ordinates approaching from the west?"

"Copied, give me a minute." Seconds later the glamorous WAAF officer came back on the air. "Come in 377, Met here."

"Reading you."

"Yes, it could be worth a try. The main front is moving away; you may get a temporary clearance. Good luck."

The dog party were in single file. Progress would have been exhausting otherwise, Sgurr acting as trail breaker and the rescuers following in his wake.

They were now in the great boulder field with the dog ranging ahead. Sgurr still had his cold light stick attached to his harness which had been activated when they left Base in the gloom of first light. This was still proving advantageous for keeping track of him as the green light rose above the drifts from time to time as he surfed through the snow.

David and Duncan were reluctant to move. The cold was biting into them and condensing. It resembled heavy cigar smoke. There were now even more icicles and David imagined they had been breeding overnight.

"I think that we had better get off our arses, doc. The lads will be out looking for us and we don't wish to give the impression of waiting for a free ride."

"Are you up to it?" There was genuine concern in David's voice.

"It can't be worse than sitting on my potty. What the hell!" Duncan exploded. "What's that!" A deafening bark shattered the seclusion of their den as the white blur of Sgurr leapt through the soft snow which blanked off the entrance. The dog was obviously overjoyed at finding his pal. Duncan had been a friend since he was a puppy and in fact the dog had found a buried Duncan many times during training.

"Hold your horses, Sgurr. Where's your bloody master?"

David had meantime exited through the dog's entry hole and almost collided with Willie Hay and the other two team members. 377 had already arrived at the search nucleus after a circuitous flight. John Simpson's hunch had proved correct and the cloud had rolled northwards as they made their approach.

In FLIR the infrared heat seeking equipment had been switched on when they flew over Glen Uiske where, suddenly, there was an array of heat spots. What really disturbed them was radiation at the bealach. Snow was rushing across the crest of the col and it looked like a Christmas card from Antarctica.

"These hot spots seem mighty strange," the Captain spoke over the intercom to his co-pilot when the MR frequency sprang to life: "377 calling Glen Dhu Base. Come in, please."

"Reading you, 377. We have located the two climbers." It was the crisp voice of Sergeant Alec MacDougall.

"377 to Base. We are close to the last call co-ordinates. Can you give the position of the missing party. We may be able to pick them up – there's a temporary lull."

"Wilco, 377." The sergeant relayed the GPS of the bivouac boulder and added, "You should be only minutes from the rescue dog party who located the climbers. Both are mobile, but one has eye injuries and will have to be flown directly to A & E."

"Copied, Base. Will keep you posted, standing by. Will recover casualties now."

The aftermath of a rescue operation has a well established routine. Next of kin are informed before any press statement is released and those rescued have the right to withhold their names from the press if they so wish. In the present case the police had a relatively easy task with no hysterical families to deal with.

The Merlin was flown directly to Aberdeen Hospital, where they have wide experience of eye damage injuries from oil rig accidents. David accompanied Duncan and for the first time noticed that he, too, had not escaped unscathed: two of his fingers were frostbitten.

After the lengthy aerial operation the Merlin had barely enough fuel to return to base and Squadron Leader John Simpson realised that there would be small chance of catching up with much needed sleep. As anticipated, his report of the FLIR location of hot spots and radiation on Bealach Uiske had not gone unnoticed at HQ: there was now an assembly of brass and ribbons in the main Operations Room, awaiting their return. This impressive subterranean structure was not just a nuclear bunker of vast proportions. It also served as a nerve centre in peace and possible war. It co-ordinated the aerial policing of the North Atlantic and world wide satellite distress monitoring.

"Good day, gentlemen," the Base Commander, Group Captain Michael Dundas, greeted the two airmen as they entered the vast space. They were still in their survival suits. No one else was in attendance. They put their bulky brief-cases on a table which was allocated to them.

"Sir," John Simpson returned. "Please excuse our attire. We didn't want to waste time."

"That's all right, Squadron Leader. We require an imme-diate debriefing."

Chapter 6

An estate in North Harris, in the Outer Hebrides, was purchased by a wealthy Russian businessman, Eugene Banderoski, an entrepreneur and marine historian. His property, Dubh Craig, of mountain lochs and moors extends to some 10,000 hectares. Aspects of his purchase pleased him greatly for there was a landing strip and some outbuildings used in the past for a basking shark hunting enterprise, later as a small, unsuccessful commercial airport. There is a sheltered harbour and one of the buildings is now used as a hangar. An accomplished pilot, Eugene's other passion was marine salvage.

He claimed his forefathers traded Black Sea ports before druids set up their God business at the nearby standing stones of Callanish. The Russian was a graduate of Gorky Ural State University and later spent several months freezing in a St Petersburg prison for illegal possession of state historical artefacts. His large fortune had been accumulated with the purchase of oil rights during the collapse of the Russian economy and though not the most wealthy of the oligarchs, he liked to think that he did quite well. His taste for taking risks was undiminished, as was a profound distrust for law and order.

The highland retreat was not a flight of fancy. He had several projects under way, one of which was the salvage of a Spanish galleon from the Armada, which, after evading the Elizabethan Navy by running up the east coast of Scotland and through the Pentland Firth, succumbed to rocks in a violent storm. This was thought to be just a few hundred metres west of Dubh Craig. Work had already commenced and, recently, a sunken wreck had been located and his diving crew was engaged in a survey. All his staff were Russian, several were ex-naval divers and ex-Spetnaz.

Lairds with strange traits, cults and hobbies are nothing new in these parts. Some years ago, a landlord banned anyone landing on his island on which he had built a modern castle, with baths fitted with pressurised water jets, an archenteron blasting out Handel and vases tall enough to accommodate a Maasai warrior.

When Eugene took over the estate two years previously he paid off the employees: Alec McGuire, who acted as caretaker, two gamekeepers and a housekeeper. As Dubh Craig is so remote his generous severance payment was accepted without a Gaelic murmur. Such is the power of cash.

When the Merlin had vibrated on to the Aberdeen helipad, the busiest in the world, Duncan was wheeled to the waiting ambulance. Dr David, considered as walking wounded, climbed in after his friend and sat down on the spare stretcher shelf opposite, alongside a paramedic.

"I have friends here, Duncan," David confided. "If they can't cure you, no one can."

"Aye," his pal returned, adjusting the bandages over his eyes. "Then I'll put the white stick on hold."

Fifteen minutes later they were ushered and wheeled respectively into the ophthalmic operating theatre, where a consultant was waiting.

"This is a colleague of mine, Duncan, John Black. We used to climb together at Lochnagar."

"Hi, doc. Excuse me for not shaking your hand, but I wouldn't know where to start."

A staff nurse came over and, after placing Duncan on a chair, started to unwind his dressing.

John Black turned to David. "I heard over the radio of your accident and told Angus Macleod. He'll see you at A & E. Dare I risk a pun and say that he is a dab hand with frostbite. Apparently, he did learn something at Halley Research Station other than spooking penguins."

"Oh, it'll be fine, John. I'm a minor case, but I'll be up for clinical negligence if I don't report my sins."

"Call before you leave and I'll have some news on Duncan. It's good to see you again."

"I'll be out for last orders, David, not last rites," Duncan chuckled.

It was about two hours later that Dr Bell returned to John Black's tiled halls. The eye man had just removed his mask and was pulling off surgical gloves. "That hand of yours could be a contender for the Turner prize," he observed.

"At least it won't get cold now," David grinned. "I'll take most of the wrappings off in the morning – I'm a great believer in fresh air."

"Come over to my office and have a coffee and I'll give you the low-down on your pal."

Once in the privacy of his sanctum, he motioned his friend to a seat. John's face now had a serious look. He switched on the hot water jug.

"Tell me what happened on your perambulations

yesterday. Duncan's injuries are more attributable to a suicide bomber than a blizzard."

"Didn't the police or SAR tell you that there was an explosion?"

"No."

"Well, there was. A hell of a blast." He added, "They may be wanting to keep it quiet, but it was obvious that you were going to find out."

"The blinding scenario is a bit strange," John spoke, choosing his words, "but we will leave that aside for the moment." He paused to fill two cups from an agitated jug and added instant coffee and milk. "Now, Dave, I can't remember after all these years if you take sugar?"

"Two lumps."

"Well." The consultant handed his friend a large mug which had Buddha's all-seeing eyes hand-painted round the circumference. "As you are well aware, explosion emits a very bright light, causing macular blindness, an oedema which recovers after a few weeks."

"And?" David prompted.

"The other possibility is that the explosion, due to the sudden pressure wave, caused bilateral vitreous haemorrhage. In both cases rest, eye pads and systemic steroids are treatment options, which have now commenced."

"Long term?"

"He should be right as rain in a few weeks."

Both doctors were silent as they sipped their coffee and John took up the subject again. "Let's talk big bangs, Dave. While Angus Macleod was sunning himself in Antarctica I was re-assembling victims from the Falls Road in Belfast and later in Kandahar. I'm no stranger to blast trauma." "It was quite an explosion, considering it was competing with a force 9 blizzard."

"I see," John ruminated.

David continued, feeling the eyes on his mug disconcerting; one, he thought looked bloodshot. "The light and blast were intense. I was some way behind Duncan at that point – the pressure centre was possibly just ahead of him."

"Could it have been a plane pranging in the bad weather, a military one?" He continued, "It almost looks like the symptoms of a dirty bomb or depleted uranium. We had better see if you got any contamination."

"Good God, man. I come in for a cup of tea and you tell me that I could be radio active!"

"Certainly active, Dave. I think that the dramatic blizzard would have acted as an effective filter."

"I just don't know, John. I was suffering from mild hypothermia and then flattened by the blast. There was only a glow afterwards. I suspect that I must have been partially blinded, too. It was both diffused and confused by the snow."

"I have been interested in explosive devices since I first qualified," his friend ruminated. "Did you know that the Chinese were the first to develop a land mine? This may have been as early as 1277 AD. It's said that it was invented by Lou Qianxia in the days of the Song Dynasty." There was a note of enthusiasm in his voice and his eyes had a far away look. "We think of home-made bombs from Afghanistan, Balkan and IRA campaigns, the fertiliser jobs, but the formula for the early Chinese devices, if I remember correctly, was:

1 lb of white sandalwood powder
3 oz of iron rust – ferric oxide
5 oz of white charcoal powder which came from quick lime
2 oz of willow charcoal powder
6 oz of dried, ground and powdered dates
3 oz of bran."

"How the hell did you remember that, that vegetarian cocktail," David spluttered.

"Simple. I manufactured it once upon a time as a party surprise, but by luck I had a rehearsal and demolished my greenhouse."

"Good God, man. You should be locked up. You haven't changed. I remember now some of your madcap ideas at uni."

"Before you go, David." John gave a wide grin. "Tell me about your friend. He seems a tough cookie." He put his feet on a nearby chair.

"He did a lot of climbing, from an early age, I gather, and served in 45 Commando and Special Services. I don't know much about that but he turned up in a small cottage about forty miles from where he lives now. Quite recently, he inherited Inverstack Estate from a distant aunt he barely knew. Remarkable! I thought that it was a disappointment for him in some ways, for he liked to poach for the old people of the village where he lived until the inheritance. After he moved, he got bored with legal stalking and salmon fishing and now leases both through an agency. Another thing, he's a bit of a detective and solved a murder case which had the police forensic team baffled. You may recall," David had a tone of admiration in his voice, "a minister who was a member of the same mountain rescue team as Duncan and was murdered when his motor cycle was tampered with on the way to a call-out."

"I remember," John put in. "It was plastered all over the papers."

"That's it. Quite an interesting deduction on Duncan's part and he was lucky not to be a victim himself."

David stood up.

"Before you go, David, I'll ring up our radiology

department and they'll give you a frisk. We have a number of cases we deal with here, usually minor from nuclear power stations. We will check out Duncan afterwards."

David's departure was delayed but his levels were normal and the senior radiologist agreed with John Black that the curtain of snow travelling at 120 kph saved his bacon. The doctor was allowed to go home and dropped in to say goodbye to John.

"Looks as if I'm clear, John. Thanks for your help, advice and coffee. My secretary is on the way to collect me." He held out his un-bandaged hand. "Keep me posted as to when Duncan is fit to be taken home."

"I'll do that. He'll need rest and attention for a while and I expect that I'll have a visit from Special Branch as well as from the local police."

"More form filling," David responded.

As they reached the door, John commented, "I took samples from Duncan's skin and clothing and I'll give you my prognoses in due course."

"Let's hope that it will be less dramatic than your greenhouse bomb – stick to your day job!"

The next morning there was a bustle of activity in the region of Bealach Uiske. Though the weather had eased, it still made flying hazardous. Ground troops, as RAF mountain rescue teams are often called, were dropped off as far up the glen as possible, just beyond the large boulder field, and they dug their mountain tents into drifts and set up base from which to operate in a white world of spindrift. They are past masters at making a home-from-home in the most hostile environments.

Meantime, the boffins back at the Co-ordination Centre had gone through the FLIR records and telephone files repeatedly and a red alert had been issued on this evidence.

Satellite and AWAK pictures had been studied in minutia to establish if an aircraft, or perhaps even a missile, had been involved, but with a return to 98 per cent cloud cover nothing further was found. The evidence from the Merlin's FLIR which was of a new, advanced type, was positive and the trauma of the two reliable witnesses irrefutable. Whitehall had been informed and three anti-terrorist officers were being flown to RAF Lossiemouth by military aircraft, as well as inspectors of Air Accidents Investigation Branch (AIB).

Unaware of these events in the north of Scotland, Derek and Michelle had made their way via the Channel Tunnel to Cambridge in a leisurely fashion, considering their mode of transport. Now Derek's Mercedes was parked outside Michelle's flat close to the university and he was awaiting her return. She had gone to college to meet with her professor, Eustace Mir.

On impulse, he unpacked his gear and, taking his laptop to the desk in the corner of the room, plugged it in as the battery was low. He went to the kitchenette and made a coffee, then looked appreciatively over her large lounge, though he had seen it many times. She had put her stamp on it with fine paintings, some belonging to her father, and an expected array of archaeological artefacts. An antique Persian rug dominated one wall and picked up highlights on its silken sheen. He returned to the desk and sat down, deep in thought. As he sipped the hot drink a furrow appeared on his brow, a signal of worry on his usual carefree appearance. He had had this premonition before, usually before an unpleasant event and mainly during his time in the Special Services or on a big climb which had gone wrong.

As he raised the lid of the laptop he felt he was about to open another chapter in this scenario. He required assistance and, like the ex-French Foreign Legion, all he had to do was pick up the phone or send an e-mail and help would be at hand, no matter how long ago you left active service ranks.

"Hi, I'm in the UK at present and may even descend on you in a few days. As usual, I seek advice, harking back to our climbing days when we didn't care a damn – or anything else! I know that you don't normally start to climb a sea stack from bedrock, but I look for such a pinnacle which rests upon several legs. I can guess your comment... 'The bugger has been too long in the sun!' However, I have a genuine motive in my search, so if you can stir your brain box, let me know? What about our mutual friend partial to life below the ocean waves? The ever elegant 'M' sends her salaams."

He shut down the computer and went through to the kitchen. He was now engrossed in preparing a meal when Michelle stormed into the flat. She put a brief case and her laptop on a sofa and discarded a fine silk scarf with gay abandon.

"Ah, what would I do without my personal slave?" She wrapped her arms round him, undoing the rear ties of the jazzy apron he had commandeered. "What I do need is a mute eunuch that can't speak back or make demands. Seriously, such features would improve you no end. Do I detect an exotic eastern dish?" She peered into the steaming saucepan, "or is there some subterfuge?" She put her hand over his which was holding a wooden spoon. With her heel she pressed open the pedal of the waste bin and glanced inside. "Ah, I thought so, the aluminium foil of an M & S Instant Curry. I thought you were just too good to be true. I'll have my shaman transform you into a dumb waiter instead of a sham eunuch!"

"If you don't want it, you know what to do," and he

added with a laugh. "That dad of yours spoiled you with official banquets."

"Now, now, Derek," she pouted and, raising both his hand and the spoon, tasted the concoction. "Yum, this is great. I'll let you keep your balls after all!"

Chapter 7

Duncan had two official visits when he was still under Dr Black's jurisdiction. The first was from Special Branch, a couple of officers in plain clothes. They sat on chairs either side of the bed and in a purposeful, yet conversational way, elicited every fragment of information from the start of the climb on the West Ridge of Beinn a'Glo to the time of the explosion in the blizzard. They were not distracted by Duncan's eye dressings. Duncan recognised the voice of one of them. He could partially see him as there was a slight gap to the side of his left eye dressing. It was as if the policeman had read his mind.

"I've seen you at some of the Highland Games, Duncan. Are you still competing in the 'heavy events'?"

"No, I'm more of a spectator now, not because of these bandages, I may add, but the only event these days is dragging myself up some mountain or other."

"It's more athletic than tossing the caber, though," the policeman responded.

"Correct," the team leader replied, "but less dynamic, as they say."

Sometime later, after Duncan had been fed a semi-liquid lunch by a stern Aberdonian nurse, three anoraks were shown into the small private ward. They were a different kettle of fish from their predecessors, lacking the humanity of the Special Branch officers. All had hard eyes of men who had witnessed suffering and perhaps even perpetrated it. Their recent uncomfortable flight from south west England on a military aircraft had perhaps emphasised this. They didn't mess about and didn't sit down. Duncan placed them as from a Special Services branch, knowledgeable and ruthless. One of them, unlike his companions, was wearing a tie with his military camouflage. He was the first to speak.

"We have your dossier, MacGilivery. You are, or were, almost one of us."

He looked down at the team leader who was propped up on a couple of pillows, apparently unconcerned that he was addressing a mummified head.

"Not quite," Duncan returned, with a muffled edge to his voice. "I was at the sharp end. You'd know that if you served behind the ridges in Yemen."

"Our activities are somewhat different, as you can probably guess, but our objectives have a common aim."

Another anorak cut in. He was swarthy, with a public school accent. "We are particularly interested in the helicopter you saw when you were climbing."

"I was, too," Duncan retorted, adjusting an edge of one of his face bandages so that he had a somewhat better blurred image.

"How about running through the whole incident from when you first heard the helicopter to the time of the explosion. We will take a recording and ask some questions afterwards, if required."

The so far silent member of the trio, like a conjuror,

produced a small digital recorder from his anorak pocket and switched it on.

"OK."

It took Duncan fifteen minutes to go through the series of events and he was very thorough and his voice didn't falter.

"We got that, MacGillvery, very professional." It was the tie man again. He was obviously the senior member of the group. "I have some further questions regarding the identification of the helicopter and my two friends, who are experts in their own fields, will want details on the explosion and the aftermath."

All this took about a further half hour and the dialogue was interrupted by the entry of Dr John Black who looked angry. Apparently, a flustered nurse had reported to him that his patient was being badgered by the visitors.

"This interview is now terminated," he barked. "You were clearly informed that my patient is still in recovery from severe trauma as well as post-operational stress and I don't like to find this trust abused. Can you please leave immediately." He glared at the men who were taken aback. Only the tie boss offered an explanation as they sidled to the door.

"We have a duty to investigate all possibilities of this incident, doctor; there are aspects of the explosion which we must establish."

"You will receive the report on my patient in the next few days," the doctor retorted. Without another word the three left as inconspicuously as they had arrived.

Two days later Duncan approached Inverstack, his inherited estate house, an imposing building with six slated turrets. It had thirty-two rooms, many unused. He was being driven by David Bell, now with a more manageable dressing on his frost bitten hand.

"Do you miss your wee cottage, Duncan?" The doctor

gave him a quick glance. They were half way up the long avenue of sequoias from the main road. He was driving carefully here for the snow was still hard packed even though the main roads were clear. Duncan gave a long pause as if deliberating an important speech.

"Sometimes I do and sometimes I don't, David. I feel that I could do more back at my old cottage. My cat died a short time before I moved in here. That put a damper on things. By the way, when am I allowed to see again? It's a bit boring, like a protracted power cut." Duncan's small inspection slit had already been covered over again by the doctor who gave a laugh.

"John Black asked me to keep an eye on you, so to speak; that was the condition of your release."

"Ah, well, in that case perhaps you could check my e-mails. I haven't looked at my computer for days."

"Sure."

The doctor had taken the precaution of telephoning Inverstack to inform Mrs Mathieson, Duncan's elderly house-keeper, of her boss's imminent return and as they swung on to the expanse of snow-covered gravel in front of the house he saw her, dressed in battleship grey, standing under the grand sandstone entrance, as upright as the support pillars but as thin as a lath.

"Good Lord, man," she addressed her laird as he got out of the car, obviously taken aback at the bandages. "And you, too, doctor, with that hand of yours. Have you been in some brawl again?" She looked genuinely shocked. "How in the good Lord's name could you get those injuries in the worst blizzard for years? Are you blinded?"

"Auch dinna fash yersel, woman." Duncan exclaimed, with a laugh. "It's only a wee accident I've had and the doctor here has an excuse not to play his pipes."

After an abridged version of their adventure as Duncan was led through the hall by David, the ritual fussing of the housekeeper subsided when they entered the drawing room and she scuttled away, only to return minutes later as if by magic, with a trolley laden with hot scones and ritual tea in a large ornamental pot. The two men subsided into deep armchairs placed at tolerance range from an enthusiastic log fire in a wrought iron basket. High brass fire fenders ricocheted flashes of yellow light and a statuary royal stag's head graced the over-mantel. Despite its size the oblong room had a cosy feeling. On the floor was a large oriental carpet uncluttered by furniture which was placed tastefully round the perimeter. After Mrs Mathieson had hovered and reluctantly departed, they had their fill of scones and honey and moved to Duncan's adjoining study.

"You don't need a rope to keep check of me, now, Dave. I can see my way by looking down my nose like a guardsman and, incidentally, I'm not glowing with radio activity."

Dave gave an infectious laugh. "Quite a pad you have here, Duncan. Don't you feel like Ahab without a crew?"

"Searching for that last great white mountain?"

"I was meaning the size of the place, especially after your half dram cottage."

"The computer is switched on at the mains, Dave, and to answer your question, you get used to the extra space and get exercise answering the door bell."

A couple of minutes later, David announced, "OK, Duncan, I'm wired up. Do you want me to read incoming Mail?"

"Fine. Most will be binned anyhow."

"Let me get you a perch." He took over an oak stool and put it behind his patient. He then sat down on Duncan's swivel chair and, once on line, commenced.

"Mostly junk, as you say, Duncan, but the last one is from a 'Mr Blank', know him? I'll continue, see if it makes sense."

"I know Mr Blank. Carry on."

He read Derek's message. "Do you know what it's about?" David looked at his friend and wondered why he bothered. Duncan was as inscrutable as a mummy."

"From another time, Dave."

"I know it's none of my damned business, but I find your e-mail intriguing, especially the bit about the sea stack."

"Your guess is as good as mine."

"I may be able to help. As you know, I did a lot of stack climbing with another pal of mine from Aberdeen. In fact, he was known as 'Dr Stack'."

"Go on," Duncan replied. "I'm all ears, though you can't see them."

"I went over to the Great Stack of Sanday with my friend a number of years ago. A local fisherman took us in his ten foot open dinghy with a Seagull outboard. We were wanting to have a closer look at it from the sea as we were hoping to make the first ascent. It was unusually calm – that's why Callum, the boatman, agreed to take us there in the first place."

"You're being long-winded, Dave." Duncan gave a chuckle. "If I remember correctly, the stack was first climbed by three Scottish climbers, though it had been 'got on to' by one Donald MacDonald from Lewis in the Outer Hebrides in 1876. He was a bird man, an islander who went down sea cliffs on horsehair ropes to gather gull's eggs which were part of their diet. They climbed in their bare feet, but as the stack was too difficult for Donald to climb from the sea, he had the cunning plan of spanning the top of the stack with a 300 metre long rope. As you know, Dave, the channel has been sculptured out of the Torridonian sandstone of Sanday Island by the Atlantic scooping away at the stack. It's a mini island in its own right and the cliff beyond runs along to a protruding headland. This freak of nature allowed him to take rope in a semi-circle round the edge of the moat formed between the island and the head-land. There Donald and his mates flicked it so that it lay over the top of the stack and it was tensioned and tied off. MacDonald subsequently went over the shorter gap hand over hand, with a hundred metre drop below and got rid of a colony of greater black backed gulls. He had been com-missioned by the then residents of the island as the large birds had been depleting their source of eggs for months."

"Have you quite finished, MacGillvery? I let you ramble on as I was waiting for you to get it wrong. However, there was something that you did leave out, but of course you haven't been through that channel. Though the sea appeared to be flat calm when Callum did his circumnavi-gation, there was a long pulse in there which scared the shit out of us. I think that when one of these pulses reaches the confines of the channel it gets compressed and forms a mini tidal wave in the gap, so that we had to ward off the rock on both sides. As we exited from it, on the crest of a wave, so to speak, Callum shouted to us, 'See that hole there on the side of the stack. I'll tell you about that once we get out of the channel.' Well, Duncan, this will probably answer the question of the stacks legs, for Callum told us that when as a young man fishing round the stack in spring at the low-est tide and in a real dead calm, he noticed the top of an archway on the inside of the channel, the same one we saw fifty years later. He eased the bow under this and, lowering himself beneath the gunnels and lying on his back, he pushed backwards on the rock ceiling until the roof rose into a large chamber. In the dim light he realised that the

Great Stack of Sanday rested on five legs. At any other time of the year this manoeuvre would have been impossible in his boat. Now he was scared, for he knew that if the tide or sea rose he would be trapped, but he managed to exit, using the same technique."

"Good God, Dave. That's amazing. The chances of my asking you to check my e-mails and the fact that you were told of the incident by Callum."

"I presume your friend, Mr Blank has a reason to be anonymous, Duncan, and it may be of interest to know that Callum was drowned some time ago – not far from the stack, fishing alone one balmy evening. It was presumed that he had a heart attack and fell overboard, for he was getting on in years. Also, you know, my colleague, Dr Stack, was killed on another stack when his abseil rope broke." The doctor added, "I'm possibly the only one alive who could have answered that question about the stack with five legs, Duncan. Callum and he was not one who talked about his adventures. To him it was just a fact of nature, like the stack itself."

"Thanks for that, Dave. I may be able to tell you more later. You probably know more about stacks than I do. One further thing, before you switch off. Can you send a reply to Blank." Duncan paused a second. "Looking forward to seeing you, Duncan."

Chapter 8

It wasn't made public immediately that the cause of an explosion, injuring two rescue team members, was connected with a plane crash. Aviation accidents in the Scottish Highlands are not uncommon, even in winter, and a press release on the Bealach Uiske incident had made the national dailies as another civilian aircraft colliding with a stationary mountain in remote Scotland. It was speculated that fuel was the cause of the explosion and the fact that a rescue team leader, as well as a local doctor, had been involved now made more news than the crash itself. The normal post-crash routine is that the area is closed off and guarded until such times as Air Crash Investigators arrive and collect the bits. This can sometimes take weeks. Other than the fact that it was a civilian aircraft, possibly a twin engine Islander with only a dead pilot on board, wasn't big enough for the front page and initially there wasn't speculation as to how the two climbers were involved if they hadn't been in the plane. A search for missing aircraft in the Highlands can involve thousands of man hours. The public gets bored.

Meantime, Derek was getting bored with the confines

of the flat. Michelle departed after early breakfast to the lab and didn't return until after five. Her entrance was, as usual, arresting, with a hint of Chanel No. 5.

"Hello, big boy." She seemed to have read his thought. "Oh, you always did find the uni boring."

"Any news on the firewood, Michelle?" Her presence was such that he couldn't hide a grin.

"That's a bit more like it," she smiled. "Professor Eustace Mir has been a valuable choice in respect to marine archaeology, but I wasn't aware of his knowledge of the Crusades. In fact he was born in Jordan, in sight of Shobak, and claimed descent from the Order on his father's side." She paused.

"Well, go on," he urged.

"Though I didn't even mention it, he immediately spotted the carved cross. He exclaimed, I wonder what this Crusader cross is doing on the carving? I replied that that's one of the questions I was going to ask. He said that he would have to think about it, but wanted to finish the infra red tests to end the day; we haven't completed them yet. That brings you up to date."

"At least things are moving," he replied. "But what did he say about the carving?" He looked at her intently, worried that the whole thing would be rubbished and that the prof was being kind in showing interest.

"Oh, don't worry, Derek. He's a man of science and if he thought it a wild goose chase he would have said. I think that you found something significant chasing that green lizard."

The following morning, after saying goodbye to Michelle, Derek set off in his car. He knew he had to consult with his friends in Scotland. Michelle realised that this was pending and promised to join him when she had completed the tests.

It was late evening when Derek eased the Mercedes up the drive leading to Inverstack. The trees were outlined black against the lights from the bay windows and floodlights. Above the snow-splattered lawn, dark silent peaks were uplifted like ghosts preparing for a nocturnal outing.

Mrs Mathieson answered the door bell. "Yes?" she greeted the tall man in an abrupt voice, a tone usually reserved for tradesmen and travelling evangelists, even though she realised that this was beyond their normal operating hours and that this man had been to the house previously.

"I'm expected by Duncan MacGillvery." Derek gave her a broad grin.

She defrosted and, reluctantly, said, "Oh, you had better come in," adding, "Mr Duncan did say that someone was coming, but he didn't say it was at nine o'clock."

The now bandage-free laird appeared in the doorway opposite the hall. "Come in, Derek. You're a sight for my poor eyes."

"You look as if you have been in an arson attack." Derek went over and grasped his friend's hand. "Good God, what have you been up to?"

"Good God indeed," Mrs Mathieson echoed as she stamped out to the servants' quarters.

"Oh, don't bother with the cailleach – the old woman to you," Duncan laughed. "Her bite is worse than her bark. Come into my den and I may produce a good fire and a dram which is made from the 'tears of the angels', as the distillers say."

"You'll never change, Duncan. Here you are, king of your inherited castle, and your opening sentence is virtually a confession and a violation of excise laws."

"You always were one for havering, Hawthorne, or do you go under another name these days?" He gave Derek a bloodshot glance from under what once were eyebrows.

Duncan went over to a cabinet to the side of the fireplace

and produced two cut crystal tumblers and opened a rather old looking bottle. Taking these in one large hand, he put them and the bottle on an upright log by the hearth. "Sit you down, man. We have talking to do. I'll tell you about my mishap later."

"I'm retired like you and, yes, I still have my family name." Duncan poured some malt and handed a glass to his friend. "Thanks. But I didn't land on my feet like you."

"Don't give me any camel shit! You arrive in a three hundred grand set of wheels and have a girl who some men would die for."

Duncan took an old battered bayonet, his poker, and re-assembled the logs in the grate. There was a silence disturbed only by the attack of kindling on silver birch logs. Beside Derek's chair Mrs Mathieson had parked a mini buffet trolley. Derek selected a succulent portion of cold venison (so much for not expecting anyone, he thought) and put the meat in a napkin so that the long fibres protruded, which reminded him of a shrunken head. "Your work, Duncan?"

"No," the big man replied with a sigh. "I've given up killing both humans and deer."

"Delicious," Derek exclaimed, licking his fingers. He continued. "Other than wanting to witness how the other half lives, I have a mission, as you probably gathered from my e-mail." He took a sip of the Talisker, which his friend had also inherited from his aunt, and looked across at him. He must be into his fifties, he mused, and yet looks as tough as when they were in Oman together. "I'll run through the scenario and you can ask questions when I finish, OK?"

"Shoot." Duncan adjusted his bulk in the armchair and leaned back, the flames throwing points of light on his inscrutable features, which at the same time showed com-passion, despite fresh scars on his face.

Derek explained how after leaving the Service he had begun to indulge his obsession with the Crusades.

Duncan had only one sip of Talisker during the detailed account and both raised their glasses. "Aye, Derek, that old soak Omar Khayyam got it right when he said: 'I often wonder what the Vintners buy one half as precious as the Goods they sell.' But I wonder what he would have written had he tasted this stuff." He added, "You know, that was interesting and I have a feeling that your bit of firewood is more than just flotsam. However, I have more news," he added, looking into the flames. His face now had a pensive look and the glint in his eye exposed a trace of excitement, a rare thing for this quiet man.

"Have I to refill your glass before you tell me?" Derek gave one of his contagious smiles accompanied with a deep laugh.

"Not at all. I was just assembling words. First, I have to confess that I also have had an interest in the Crusades, ever since we spent time in Jordan and Palestine and slept in their castles. But I'll start with your stool on legs."

Derek on the opposite side of the fireplace studied his friend with renewed interest.

"Do you remember, Derek, a Dr Dave Bell who is in the rescue team?"

"The climber?"

"Yes. He's keen on sea stacks and he told me that the Great Stack of Sanday sits on five sandstone legs, caused by erosion." Duncan looked for a reaction, but all he saw was a narrowing of Derek's eyes.

"Well, well, what do you know!"

"A bit more," Duncan returned. "I'll fill you in on what he told me." He retold the doctor's details of the sea stack almost verbatim and when he finished, he gave a smoking log a prod and it sprang to life as if it had been stabbed.

"Duncan, before we talk into the night I'd better give Michelle a ring. I've got my mobile."

"The signal's crap here, Derek. Use the phone in the hall. Meanwhile, I'll get more logs."

"Thanks."

Ten minutes later Derek was back and Duncan had freshly cut wood in a large wicker basket at arm's length from his chair.

"And how's my favourite scientist?" he asked when Derek returned.

"Fine, Duncan. She'll be up day after tomorrow. I'll collect her from the sleeper. She sends her regards."

Derek went over to raid the meals on wheels trolley again. "Want anything?"

"No, thanks. I didn't tell Dave what it was all about, but I could see that he was intrigued."

"I bet. What's the score with Jack Rippon, Duncan?"

"By coincidence he phoned three days ago. He was putting down some moorings for a friend in Assynt and was thinking of calling by with his rib and trailer on his way home. I mentioned – not to be too public on the phone – that you had an interest in the Great Stack of Sanday with a view to trying a new route on it and you had a £500 bet with a climbing friend that it was possible.

"Good thinking, Duncan. I see that you haven't lost your skills in subterfuge. But I bet that didn't fool Jack!"

"But I'm worried, Derek." A deep line cut across the new laird's forehead and he reached over for the half empty bottle. He held it up, offering a refill to Derek who raised a hand, declining.

"What about?"

"I haven't heard from him."

"Three days, you say?"

"That's right. He was definitely coming over here afterwards."

"His mobile?"

"No joy."

"What next, Duncan. You're the expert here."

"Well, he must have left his Land Rover and trailer somewhere, probably at Tebrat. That's the most likely place."

"So, we'd better check it out?"

"It could be awkward for me, as rescue team leader. I feel that I should respond in the normal way. But I think that we may be jumping the gun. You know as well as I do that Jack is a master of under-water warfare and has spent his life risk-taking. The fact that he has not turned up could be caused by a host of factors. However, you're right in saying that we should check it out and should take ourselves to Tabrat after breakfast and look for that boat trailer. If we find it but no Jack, I'll have to start the ball rolling."

"And if we don't."

"It could be just as bad. There's been a lot of strange happenings lately, Derek. Let me give you a quick run-down concerning my accident, which also involved David Bell. It probably has nothing to do with Jack and he may well come breezing in here looking for an all-day breakfast."

"Do you really believe that?"

"No, but before we hit the hay let me tell you what happened on a climb with Doc Bell and the explosion which almost wiped us off the planet."

Michelle dashed along the platform at Kings Cross Station to catch her train. She attracted admiring glances as she ran with a rucksack and her beloved computer satchel, and scrambled aboard with her dignity intact. She had left a message on Derek's voice mail earlier in the day confirming her arrival time.

The reason she hadn't managed to speak with Derek was that he had departed at first light in Duncan's Range Rover and had arrived at the cluster of stone cottages which constituted the clachan, or small hamlet, of Tebrat at about 10 am. It's an idyllic spot where the ribbon of tarmac abruptly runs out on to beach gravel and, if you are admiring the view instead of the track, you would drive into the eastern Atlantic, with the island of Sanday dead ahead.

Both men saw the boat trailer before they reached the beach. A well-used Defender Land Rover, attached to a four-wheeled trailer, was parked above high water mark. Duncan drew up alongside. The beach and the channel were hidden by rising ground between the few scattered cottages and the sea.

"Well," he muttered, "part of our quest has been fulfilled."

"But where's Jack?" Derek responded, getting out of the vehicle.

"And where's the rib?" Duncan asked. He went over and looked through the driver's window. "Just what I would expect from a Special Boat Service man – all shipshape." Derek tried the back door. It, too, was locked, as was the passenger door.

"I'll try and get him on the mobile," said Duncan. "We may have more luck here."

Derek examined the inside of the 4 x 4, holding a hand at right angles to the glass, for the sun was now streaming down. He noted a neat interior with two bunk type lockers running along the length of the sides, with a couple of large aluminium flight cases in place of rear seats. "All in order inside, Duncan," he called.

"No joy on the mobile," Duncan called back. He had moved down to the edge of the water where the tide was on the turn. "I wonder if we should try him on the Marine Band. He has a base station fitted below the dash and I know he never goes on water without a two-way radio with its own buoyancy vest. Come to think of that, I should have tried the radio back at Inverstack or from my own vehicle which also has Marine Band; we use it on call-outs for coms with navy choppers."

"It's worth a try," Derek agreed and joined him at his Range Rover. He opened the passenger door and perched on the seat. He looked at the team leader who was now obviously worried.

"Damned if I know which frequency to use. I don't want to spill any beans to the coastguard yet, but Jack may be missing. I'll try Channel 32." A terse grin animated his rugged features and Derek could see a multitude of tiny scars all over his face.

"This is five legged spider calling sponge. Come in, please." Duncan now had a twinkle in his eye and Derek gave a subdued laugh.

"It's a long time since I heard Jack called 'Sponge', Duncan."

"If he receives it, he'll know who's calling." He continued transmitting at five minute intervals, but there was no response.

"I would imagine that he would have his set on scan, Duncan, if he uses 32 for personal messages," Derek mused, more to himself.

"That's what I imagined," Duncan returned, "but there's nothing."

The excited throb of an outboard could now be heard and both men got out of the vehicle and crunched down the beach of perfectly rounded pebbles. An eighteen foot white dory circled round the rocky headland from the south, bouncing on the swell which sounded like a drum beat. It angled into the bay, barely slackening pace. There was a man at the stern. He gave a wave with his free hand. They saw he was in green oilskins with two day-glow stripes running up the arms to the upturned collar. Barely slowing, he cut the engine just as it hit shore and the twin hulled craft crunched up the beach on the ball bearing pebbles. It ground to a halt at almost touching distance.

"I see you have done this before." Duncan greeted the boatman. They noted as he stepped over the gunwale that he was tall and weather beaten, with a wide grin revealing gold fillings.

"I'm Angus Beaton," the boatman replied heartily, holding out a knarled hand which looked as if he had been hauling creels most of his life.

"This is my friend Derek. I'm Duncan MacGillvery."

"Man, I thought I recognised you, Duncan, but you seem to have been in the wars, an encounter with naphtha or a rogue barbecue? You're with the mountain rescue." He looked quizzically at the big man, then back at Derek. Both these men had a presence and seemed edgy.

"We are looking for our friend who owns the rig." Derek jerked his thumb at the Land Rover and trailer.

"I have no idea." Angus studied the trailer and Land Rover. "I have just come up from Scurbhan harbour a couple of miles away to take some tourists over to Sanday. They'll be here shortly." He paused for a moment and continued looking at Duncan with pale blue eyes. "There was a bit of a storm a couple of days ago and I saw a big rib going up the Sound when I was fishing. There was a swell rising, so I just dropped my pots and headed back home."

"The rib?"

"Oh, it couldn't have been your friend. It was big, over

nine metres, I would say, with three or four people on board. It was dark in colour. The crew were wearing dry suits – I could see their dark, wet reflections. It had, I think, two engines and I assumed that it must be Navy; nobody else could afford the fuel." He added, "it was going north slowly and close into the Sanday cliffs."

"What time was this?" Derek asked.

"About 2 pm."

"Thanks for your help, Angus. If you see our friend's boat, tell him – his name is Jack – to give me a call, otherwise we'll have to report it to the coastguard. By the way, his rib has a short, white mast and a long aerial above the console."

"I'll do that if I see him," Angus replied. "My number is Killochbevie 1256 and I'll quizz the locals."

At that moment there was the echo of a vehicle descending the single track road, then a mini bus appeared. It was canary yellow and emblazoned with the logo 'Mountains and Sea'.

"Your bread and butter has arrived, Angus," Duncan observed. "Good luck."

Chapter 9

It was midday before the London sleeper slunk into Inverness station like a reluctant snake. Derek was pleased at the delay, for the opportunity to have a coffee on the terrace of a new café in the main street which still smelled of fresh paint. There was a lot to think about in the two unexpected hours. He was worried and felt guilty, guilty in involving two of his best friends in what was rapidly escalating into a serious series of events. His only consolation was that it was obvious from Duncan's singeing that he was not wholly to blame. Jack was another matter. Jack was a model of efficiency. Everything he did had a logical pattern, yet his reactions were like greased lightning. Derek always thought that his charmed life could only be terminated by a natural disaster or a bullet. He could never imagine him growing old or getting some terminal illness. It was as if he had stumbled on a magical elixir, and the small matter when he had saved Derek's life.

After a leisurely stroll back to the station, the sight of Michelle walking along the platform was like a ray of light. He had met her a few years before in the French Alps when she had been climbing with Lucy, a girlfriend, who was also an international mountain guide. They had just completed a traverse of the Grandes Jorasses. Derek, who had been on this same traverse, was climbing solo some way behind and he greeted them on the summit of Point Walker, the highest top where they had stopped for a sandwich. It was a magnificent day, with the high Alps alive in morning sunshine.

"Derek, Derek Hawthorne." He gave them a salutation with his short ice axe. "I must be getting old," he confessed. He put on his sun glasses and realised that he was instantly attracted to the blonde one who was introduced as Michelle. Her friend was Lucy.

"We thought that we could burn you off." Michelle gave an infectious laugh, a laugh which he later got to know so well.

"Girl power and all that crap," Lucy cut in, her face almost black from a long season in the Alps. "Just as well we had sandwiches – almost Victorian, don't you think?" She offered one to Derek. "Makes the halt almost legitimate."

"Thanks." He realised that Lucy was a very fit girl.

"Did you two know each other in another life?" Lucy asked with a quizzical smile.

"Unfortunately, not," Derek laughed. "I was just thinking what I had missed." He took a bite of cucumber on French bread.

All three descended to Courmayeur on the Italian side of the mountain. Later Michelle and Derek saw each other at every opportunity. She was taking an honours degree at Cambridge and he was in the forces, based in Oman.

Now as they drove north to Inverstack they immediately relaxed in each other's company. It was as if they had blended like a good malt, mellow, yet underneath explosive. There still snow on the high tops and white camouflaged ptarmigan, with overworked wings, darting across the road just in front, thinking they were low flying jets.

They circled to a halt to the homely crunch of gravel in front of Inverstack House. Duncan was standing at the main entrance.

"Hello, Michelle, you bring an ambience of glamour and knowledge to the old house."

"Hi, Duncan." She ran over from the car to give him a hug. "My," she continued, stepping back, "you look as if you just survived a funeral pyre."

"No doubt that man of yours told you – there may be a grain of truth in your observations. But come on in. I'm sure we can get my tame Amazon to rustle up some coffee or, as she calls it, 'the beverage of the devil'."

When they were seated by a substantial fire in the bowels of the fireplace, Michelle asked her host. "Was your aunt responsible for the decor and furniture, Duncan?"

"Yes, indeed," he responded with what Derek thought was enthusiasm. "Though I hardly knew her, I find myself thinking about, say, the colour of a rug, or the way a piece of furniture is positioned in some niche in a casual yet subtle way exactly how I would have done it. It's uncanny, but then..." he gave a bellow of a laugh, "probably I'm bone idle and can't be bothered with change."

"I'm like your aunt and you, Duncan, but I'm sure that Mrs Mathieson has something to do with keeping it this way." She looked round the large room approvingly. The tinkling of bone china announced the arrival of the good lady's trolley.

"We have just been admiring the way you keep the house, Mrs Mathieson. It must be a lot of work."

"Hard work never did anyone any harm if they have a mind for it." She was obviously flattered at Michelle's compliment and, despite her arthritis, dexterously poured their coffee. She didn't usually do this and Duncan, amused at the ritual, wondered if it was the devil himself that had prepared the beverage. She gave him a quick glance as if she could read his thoughts and, when her task was completed, disappeared into the nether regions of the house.

"I haven't asked Michelle yet about the wood carving, Duncan. I thought we would get it from the horse's mouth, but I did mention to her that Jack was overdue from his boat trip – she never met him."

It was as if a dark cloud had descended on Duncan. He paused, almost in respect, before replying. "After you left, Derek, I had to report to the coastguard that he was over-due and they set the ball rolling. They have the Stornoway chopper on to it, as well as the local lifeboat and it will be a full scale emergency tomorrow. A general alert was put out and I gave them Angus Beaton's number. Also," he added as an afterthought, "I have arranged with an ex-naval colleague to have his rib at Tebrat first thing tomorrow morning. We will be able to have a look round with him."

"Good idea, Duncan," Derek muttered quietly. "But let's hope Jack makes it."

"If he does," Duncan speculated, "he will be in a vile temper over all this fuss."

Michelle, in an attempt to lighten the conversation, put down her cup and sandwich which was balanced on the saucer and reached for her laptop. "Mostly good news, boys." She looked up at them both. "With reservations. The latter is the usual noncommittal comment we inherited from lawyers, 'without prejudice' of course." She gave them another radiant smile.

"Give," Derek laughed.

"My tutor, Prof Eustace Mir, who is one of the leading

experts on marine archaeology, also has a wide knowledge
– especially of the Templars, as Derek knows. He is reasonably sure that the wood carving which Derek found is of
our period. The carved cross is very specific and all the tests
we ran established the segment of wood as a significant
artefact, however." She picked up her sandwich and, after
a nibble, placed her laptop on one of the carved side tables.
"Derek has seen some of this before, Duncan, but it will put
you in the picture."

"I see what you mean about the stool with the legs,
Derek. These are great images."

"Or the Great Stack of Sanday?" his friend added quietly.

"Further more," Michelle continued with her theme,
"infra red scans and carbon dating information suggest the
early fifteenth century – all very encouraging."

"That's great news," Derek responded. It was as if he
had just shed the demons that had been haunting him.

"Michelle," Duncan looked over at her as he removed
a small flake of skin which was parked where his left eyebrow used to be, "I was going to explain to your boyfriend,
or rather confess, as one of thousands of errant youths
world wide with a passion for the Crusades, I was smitten
much earlier than Derek." There was a twinkle in his eye.

Michelle was all attention.

"I discovered that another of my boyhood heroes came
into the agenda, King Robert the Bruce." Derek was
amused at the animation displayed by his friend and was
wondering when he was going to attack one of the logs in
the fire.

"Let me explain, for it is part of the broader canvas.
The king had been involved in a bloody skirmish with the
MacDougal clan at a place called Dail Righ, near Tyndrum.
Bruce was probably one of the greatest guerrilla fighters of

all time. The MacDougal chief had good reason to be pissed off with this warrior for he had knifed and killed his father-in-law at the high alter of Greyfriars Church, Dumfries. Later, when the Bruce was going through MacDougal land, the chief, John MacDougal, was alerted and had over one thousand clansmen, outnumbering Bruce's force three to one. The king was forced to retreat and he took up the rearguard close to Lochan nan Arm to help defend his men. But," Duncan looked at his two friends, who were obviously absorbed in this bloody history, "MacDougal's allies, the brothers MacIndrosser, managed to separate the king from his company. The first brother got hold of the bridle, the second Bruce's leg and the third leapt behind the king, grabbing his shoulder. Bruce must have been wearing armour to survive this attack. The clansman who had seized the bridle was slashed with such force by Bruce's sword that both his shoulder and arm were sliced off his body. The king then spurred his horse, dragging the assailant who had grabbed his leg, who now lost his footing and had his hand jammed in the stirrup. The pillion rider was seized by Bruce, who lifted him over his head on to the horse's neck and delivered such a blow with his sword that the man's skull was cleft to the brain and he dropped in a pool of blood. The last of the brothers, still trapped by the stirrup, was then despatched. The MacDougals were in such awe of this feat that they retreated, some openly in admiration of this remarkable warrior. But the last of the brothers to die had grabbed part of Bruce's surcoat. Pinned to this was the Brooch of Lorne, a large and beautifully worked silver ornament which is still in possession of the MacDougal clan today and is probably of eastern origin."

"That's quite a story, Duncan," Michelle breathed.

"Well, all this," Duncan replied, "is documented in

Barbour's Bruce, in my opinion one of the greatest works in the Scots language and compiled a short time after Bruce's death."

"I think that you have more, Duncan." Derek looked at his friend with admiration. Duncan could always surprise him with his interest in the most diverse subjects.

"You could be right, but first let's go back to the Brooch of Lorne. This was no ordinary ornament and could even have been Saracen. Michelle," he gave her a glance, "there may be some work to do on its origins – it's in a bank vault in London now, but I have photographs of it." She looked up with interest, but didn't reply. "Some historians think that there is evidence to suggest that Bruce may have had contact with the Templars. It's possible that he met up with them on the island of Mull and in fact his War of Independence against the English may have been partly financed by Templars, warrior monks of 'the Poor Knights of the Temple of Solomon', who had taken up residence in Scotland. This was only about seven years after they had been persecuted by, the King of France. These warriors had cropped hair and long beards with embossed surcoats. The Battle of Bannockburn was a decisive victory for the Scots, as you know, and mounted men in chain mail wearing white smocks beneath a black and white banner were seen in Bruce's ranks."

"I didn't think that you were an historian, Duncan," Michelle now cut in, obviously intrigued with Duncan's potted history. Duncan continued in centre stage.

"It was three years after the Declaration of Arbroath in 1320 that Bruce was declared by the nobles as their liege lord and Pope John XXII lifted the excommunication and recognised him as King."

"Well, Duncan, that's all very interesting, but I'm not sure if that will help us find the Templar loot."

"But you must admit that it provides that extra sense of adventure."

"I agree with you, Duncan," Michelle quickly responded. "It seems to fit in and makes the possibility of the treasure ships going to Scotland where the Crusaders knew they had an ally in Bruce. He had a cause, the War of Independence, in their interest, too, and they were well qualified to finance him and, as outstanding warriors, to lend a hand."

Chapter 10

Duncan didn't exaggerate when he said that it would be a full blown search the following morning. Two helicopters had been airborne since dawn as well as coastguard inshore craft and the same RNLI lifeboat that had been out the previous day. One RAF mountain rescue team was airlifted to the island of Sanday to check the coastline of the Inner Sound, a daunting task as the cliffs are over one hundred metres in height. Fortunately, the day was fine, with excellent visibility.

As Duncan was not officially in charge of the Glen Dhu Rescue Team due to his injuries, Wallace Dalgleish was deploying the Team on the mainland side of the Sound, opposite to where the RAF team was. They had been pulled out of the search at Bealach Uiske as all the debris from the explosion had been flown for crash analysis at Farnborough.

Duncan had asked the Commander, John Lightfoot, to assist; he had spent several years at the rocket range on St Kilda and was an expert where inflatables, ribs and big seas were concerned. He also had a large rib driven by two 100 hp Yamaha outboards. Already he was at Tebrat slip when they arrived.

"Good to see you, Duncan, pity about your friend."

"Thanks, John. These are my two companions, Michelle and Derek."

"Glad to meet you both." The Commander's voice was clipped as if he expected instant action. He was small and muscular, which was obvious even in his dry suit. He wore a naval cap which was surrounded by a wreath of blond hair squeezing under the rim. He touched this in acknowledgement with his right hand.

"I see that we are all suited up," he said, approvingly. "I still have this legacy of my naval days, Michelle." For she was approving of his smart piece of head gear. "It helps to impress if we're awash with red tape."

"I'm also impressed with your boat. It looks as if it could fly supersonic, John." She gave him one of her enthusiastic smiles.

"I took the liberty of telling the coastguard that we would be going along the base of the cliffs towards the Great Stack of Sanday, John." It was Duncan speaking as he adjusted his dry suit zip. "There will be a few private boats as well as local fishermen lending a hand. I have the MR frequencies and the maritime channels on my hand set. But you probably have these anyway."

"Not quite, Duncan, but I'm glad to see that you are as efficient as ever."

There was already a couple of 4 x 4s parked above high tide mark, one belonging to Duncan's team, which was searching the shoreline to the west. It still had its launching trolley attached.

"Let's give a hand to get this mean machine of yours into the drink," Derek volunteered.

As John reversed the trailer into the water, Duncan contacted Wallace, his deputy, to say that they would be using their eyes for the day's search, 'convalescing' on their own transport.

In minutes, the rib was afloat with Michelle and Derek aboard. John parked his trailer alongside the rescue team's wagon, then both waded out to the boat and Duncan swung a large rucksack on board. It was a Saturday morning and there was a good response for the search. Several flotillas of sea kayaks from an outdoor centre, under the eagle eyes of their instructors, had diverted schedules to enable them to take part.

The previous day, when Angus Beaton returned home, he mentioned over dinner that he had been keeping a wary eye for a missing inflatable. His twelve year old son, Magnus, a clone of his father, minus gold teeth, was pestering his dad with questions.

"Where do you think he's gone, Dad?"

"Don't you be getting any ideas, young man," his mother cut in reprovingly, putting a bowl of potatoes on the pine-wood table. "Your father has work to do."

"That's right, Magnus. I have two trips to Sanday and I'll be searching afterwards with Conservancy Rangers in the boat." He stabbed a potato from the dish and looked at his son. "But to deal with your question. The chance is that if Jack Rippon capsized in that storm from the north west and with drift, he could possibly have ended up on the coast right here. You could have a look along the shore line in the morning, but don't do anything stupid." Magnus' eyes lit up. "And," Angus raised his fork, "ask your mother if you can borrow her mobile and be sure to keep in touch."

The sea was kind with a sleepy, rock-a-bye swell. The rib was travelling at walking pace, no frenzy of revs. The four on board had binoculars. John Lightfoot was sitting as on horseback on the control consul, grasping the wheel with one hand. Duncan was behind, his bulk emphasised by his jet black dry suit.

"Duncan." It was John. "I seem to know the name, Jack Rippon. You say he's ex-Navy." He glanced sideways at the big man quizzically.

"That's right, he was with the Special Boat Service."

"Ah, I recall now," said John, slapping the side of his leg with his free hand. "Yes, dropping his boat off our corvette on an anti-pirate raid on Somalia."

"That sounds like him," Duncan agreed. "Hand to hand with pirates would be right up his alley."

"Hey, you guys, look on the cliff top." Michelle pointed, raising her binoculars. "That must be the RAF team." With the naked eye, a regular line of figures was outlined against the blue, seemingly on the very edge of the cliff.

"Quite a turn out," Derek observed. "Jack would have been proud but, come to think of it, he would cringe."

"Yes." Duncan added, looking at a member of the RAF team with his 7x50 glasses. "At one time our forefathers used to respond to a fiery cross rushed through the glens to summon help. Now it's RT and satellite phones."

"By my reckoning, the Great Stack should be directly ahead," Derek suggested.

"Do you think that's a good place to have a serious look?" It was John who asked and looked round at this quiet man with the prominent scar. John was now suspicious after his years in the Navy that he may be in the company of individuals who were not what they first appeared. He sensed a hardness, a concentration of purpose in his new crew.

"A good idea," Duncan chimed in. "I told Coastguard Control that we would be in the area of the stack, but we haven't been allocated an official search box."

"Have you any idea of where he was planning to go, Duncan?"

"No, he was up north on a mooring contract and arranged to call on his way south. It was only when he didn't turn up that I looked into it."

"Knowing Jack's insatiable curiosity and that he was a climber, it's more than likely that he would take the opportunity to have a look at the Great Stack," Derek reminisced. "He climbed the Old Man of Hoy a couple of years ago. Is that the stack you can just see ahead, blending in with the cliffs?" They all looked.

"Yes," Duncan agreed. "The gap from the stack to the rock wall of the island is only a few metres wide in places."

Just then the swish-swish beat of a Merlin helicopter was heard above the outboards. It, too, was making a sweep of the Sound and on the water, from the other direction, the local lifeboat was heading south parallel to the west shore like a diligent drugs dog checking every bit of flotsam en route. The rib chugged slowly round the side of the stack up which is the only climb. Duncan pointed it out.

"Do you see that dark overhang about halfway up?" He pointed towards the centre of the Torridonian sandstone wall. "That's the crux of the route."

"The start looks awkward," Derek observed. "You would have to step off the bow of the boat right on to hard rock."

"I've never done it," Duncan confessed.

"I think I'll stick to the sea," John laughed. "What about you, Michelle?" He looked at her eager face. A wonderful specimen, he thought; rough diamond Derek was a lucky blighter.

"I'd love to have a go," she replied, "provided someone else led."

The boat nosed its way along the base of the stack and they could see vertical rock fluting ten metres below in green crystal water. Eventually, the wall gave way to a narrow gap, not even the width of the boat. The opposing walls rose over a hundred metres, narrowing to a slot above which was turquoise sky. John eased the craft into the entrance and they felt a sudden motion, which they had not previously noticed, an up and down force which was probably where the surge was generated by the ocean, compressing it into the narrow defile. John gently eased the rib astern.

"What was that parable about the 'eye of a needle'?" Derek asked.

"Don't worry. I had no intention of chancing my luck." John laughed. "I hope your pal Jack was equally prudent."

"He didn't meet up with Davy Jones with a mistake like that," Duncan replied quietly.

As they moved back, they got a better view of the channel to where it turned left, leaving ahead the blank red wall of the island rearing like a primeval monster. There they could see a swell rising in small waves moving forward in rhythm.

"That's cool," Michelle exclaimed, pointing. "Just look at the hundreds of sea birds." She held a hand over her eyes as a shade to get a better view of the crowded ledges of the stack. "With their black and white suits, it looks like first night at the opera."

"I can give you a few facts on the bird life, Michelle. I did some swotting last night," Duncan offered.

"Go on, you big swot. You're going to tell us, anyway." She made a face at him.

"Well," he looked back at the stack's residents, "there's an assortment of wild life and this is the centre for seabirds in north west Scotland. Though it's not yet the height of the breeding season, later the ledges can be so packed with brown guillemots and black razorbills that they virtually cover the face of the rock. There is also a pecking order, with kittiwake colonies closer to the water. If I remember correctly, there are 800 puffins, 4,000 fulmars, 12,000 razorbills, 14,000 kittiwake and approximately 60,000 guillemots. It's one of the highlights of this paradise of ours."

"I thought that you had outgrown your fascination with birds." Derek gave his friend a mock punch. "But you must have a few hormones left under that sleek black suit of yours."

As they continued, the rock overhung like a partly lowered drawbridge. It felt ominous. Derek, who was up in the bow, had been taking shots of their progress. He called to John. "Can you bring the nose on to this black kelp? I'd like to take a few shots."

"Sure, Derek." He added, "I see that you're familiar with the technique of holding a rib against a rock face with engine power. We did that a lot on St Kilda for gaining access to the cliffs." He nudged the boat forwards directly on to the barnacled rock.

"Thanks, I got a good selection," Derek called. "What a fantastic texture that seaweed has." John shifted into reverse and in seconds they were away from the cliff.

The Merlin, which had been doing its routine back and forward sweep for the last hour or so, now appeared above and just ahead. Duncan, who had his walkie-talkie on scan, got a message from the pilot.

"This is the skipper of 377 calling rib directly below. Are you reading me?"

Duncan raised the mike and replied. "Loud and clear 377. Over."

"377. I presume that's Duncan MacGilivery. Coastguard told us that you were up here by the Great Stack. Duncan, further along the cliff edge is a geo, starting as a cave which opens up inside and is minus a roof which leaves a hundred metre deep hole from the surface of the island. We assume that it only floods at high tide – at least it's partly dry inside at present. Have you got that so far?"

"Yes, 377. Carry on."

"377 to Duncan. Our winch man spotted something which could be an old piece of black tarpaulin obscured by the inside arch of the geo. It might be worth investigating." He added, "It's a bit dodgy to do such a long winching operation down the inside."

"Wilko. Will check out and report back."

"377 to rib. We will take this opportunity to refuel and will return in approx. one hour. Out."

Chapter 11

So far, there were various 'finds' over a wide area of coastline: a rubber dinghy off the north end of Skye, which was probably a lost tender from a yacht, as well as bits of flotsam which were already in the hands of the coastguard and would be further checked back at headquarters.

Twelve-year-old Magnus Beaton was enjoying himself. He had thought of going to watch a shinty match, but the chance of taking part on a call-out stirred his blood. As well as his mum's mobile he had the old binoculars for his dad had taken the best ones. He also had two treacle scones and a bottle of Iron Bru, the colour of which matched his hair. He had just succumbed to the temptation of these when he picked up the binoculars to look for his dad's boat, but got distracted by a Merlin helicopter flying very low towards him. He gave a wave as it thundered overhead. As he raised the binoculars again to the task in hand, he saw a flash of light in the water just below where he was sitting. At first, he assumed that it was a bottle and a thought ran through his mind that it could be an old message from St Kilda, fifty miles west in the Atlantic. At one time, if there was an illness on the island, the residents would put an urgent note for a doctor in a bottle and throw it into the water. Invariably, it would be washed up on the west coast of Scotland and, with luck, some beachcomber would find it before the person died.

It didn't look like a bottle, but as he re-focussed the binoculars' zoom, he thought it was a small black box with a glass cap. Leaving the binos and his small day sack, he rushed down the rocky shoreline and waded into the sea, cold despite the so-called Gulf Stream.

As he fished out the object from languid waves, he realised it was a camera, but floating in a plastic pouch filled with water. He had heard of waterproof cameras, but he realised that it was past its use-by-date, with the lens smashed and a gash on the casing. Disappointed, he moved back up the beach, thinking it hadn't been worth getting his feet saturated. When he got up to his sea thrift bowrie, he took off his boots and wrung his socks in disgust.

John had his rib at the geo in minutes. It looked like the opening of a large sea cave, ten metres across and five metres high. It was low tide and the water appeared to be about half way up the entrance. This was confirmed as he tentatively took the rib under the archway. His echo sounder had moved from fifty metres to two metres. The roof was dull red. There was little seaweed on the rock and ahead they could see the channel. The cave lowered and veered left, obscuring the view, but there was light beyond; the open roof of the geo couldn't be far ahead.

"I'll swim," Derek volunteered, "and take the end of a rope. If there's anything of interest you will be able to haul it out." He sensed that John wasn't that keen on going further.

"Sounds logical," Duncan agreed. "You could take a couple of waterproof bags with you in case you find something else. I have them in my rucksack."

"I'll go with you, Derek, you might need a hand," Michelle cut in. "Duncan can act as the hauler – in case we do find that bit of tarpaulin."

"Seems sensible," John agreed, "but don't waste time for the tide is turning.

"Fine by me," Duncan said. "I'd better continue convalescing or I'll be in trouble." Already, he was opening his rucksack and took out two large sealed waterproof bags and a fifty metre length of climbing rope. In seconds, Derek had the bags tied round his waist. He dropped the coils on to the deck.

"I'll give a couple of tugs if we want a pull, Duncan."

"OK."

"Let me have about half the rope length, Michelle, before you follow in case it snags. This rope floats."

This took no more than three minutes and Duncan paid it out. John watched approvingly and confirmed his earlier conclusion that these men had a past with ingrained efficiency and no unnecessary movements were used. Derek had almost reached the bend in the tunnel when Michelle went over the side. She had a snorkel mask on her neoprene hood. Though she was a powerful swimmer, she took considerably longer than Derek to reach the bend. John and Duncan watched as they disappeared, the rope still snaking out. It stopped.

When Michelle swam round the corner, she found that she was in a large sea pool with Derek just ahead on a rock ledge to the left. Behind him was a black rib tethered on four ropes, two from the bow and two from the stern, each anchored from pitons on their respective sides of the pool. As it was low tide, these were almost tight, but even at high water the movement of the boat would be restricted.

"Hi, Michelle. I might have known that Jack would use a unique way to park his boat to remain incognito."

"Is this Jack's rib, then?" She clambered up on to the ledge beside him with a look of amazement on her wet face. She drew a gloved hand across it.

"I'm afraid so," he said grimly. "I expected as much."

"Oh, God," she exclaimed. "I feel there's a jinx of our adventure, Derek." He didn't answer.

"Michelle, we'll swim over to it and attach our rope to the bow, then release the anchor ropes. You stay aboard and I'll swim and guide it round the corner while Duncan pulls. OK?"

"Right."

"Let's go."

They both slid into the cold green water. The subdued light was eerie though it was getting brighter now. Derek swam round the back of the rib and from there could see sky above, but it was well hidden from above by overhanging rock. This, no doubt, was the reverse view of that from the Merlin. When they were on board, Derek untied the end of the climbing rope and dropped the two yachting bags on the deck, where accumulated water was swilling around. He quickly went to the bow and tied his rope to a large D ring to which two of the tether ropes were anchored. He managed to untie these and let them slip overboard and called to her to do the same with the two stern ropes.

While she was busy, he opened a waterproof locker at the side of the central consul, just below the controls and looked inside. There were several items, some in waterproof bags, and flares, a torch and charts. He grabbed one of the waterproof bags and stuffed the contents inside and quickly sealed it.

"Derek, I untied the ropes – and lost a bloody nail in the process."

"Good, but sorry about the nail. Now come up to the

bow and give Duncan's rope a couple of tugs. That should wake the blighter up. I'll be at the stern, overboard, if you need me."

She went forward on the other side of the consul, took up her position at the bow and immediately gave the climbing rope two hefty pulls. Meantime Derek was in the water hanging with both hands onto the outboard drive casing which was in the raised position.

"The rope's gone tight."

"Great," he called, kicking out to give some forward momentum. The operation worked; even getting round the corner wasn't too difficult, but he had to change over to the other side of the outboard to get sufficient paddling effect.

"Hello, Duncan," Michelle yelled. "Keep pulling, we've got Jack's rib."

"I got that." Duncan's call came thunderously through the tunnel, bouncing on its echo. Minutes later, the engines of John's rib rose to a subdued throb. It moved forward and the rope went taut, causing water spillage over the stern board which caught Derek. He clung on, but they were hardly moving and he managed to scramble aboard.

Once clear of the cave and in open water, John throttled back and made a wide circular turn to Jack's rib to avoid snagging the propellers. Duncan coiled up the rope in the stern. The boats closed in. He put a hitch over one of John's side cleats, then helped Michelle out. Her finger was still bleeding and John gave her a dressing from his first aid kit.

"No need for disinfectant in this part of the world, Michelle. There's enough salt for every chip shop in Scotland."

"Thanks, John."

Duncan called from the stern. "A first class job, you two, but it doesn't look too good for Jack."

"No sign?" John asked, returning to the wheel.

"Nothing," Derek stated, pushing Jack's rib clear. "I presume you want to tow it back, John?"

"Before we do anything, I'd better contact the coast-guard," Duncan said and picked up his radio from the scuppers.

"Duncan MacGillvery calling Coastguard Base. Come in, please."

"Reading you, Duncan, pass your message."

"As you know, 377 asked us to check the sighting of black material in a geo, just north of the Great Stack. We managed to recover the missing rib there, inside the geo and now have it in tow. We await instructions. Over."

"Coastguard Control to Duncan. Stand by. Over."

John now with a smile took the opportunity and produced a large flask of coffee and a box of chunky sandwiches.

"You're a magician, John," Michelle enthused. "I was just thinking about a hot drink. That was like having a dip in an ice floe." She pointed with a newly plastered finger.

They were all sitting on the rib's side tubes when the radio woke up.

"Coastguard Control to Duncan. Come in, please."

"Pass your message."

"Can you proceed south down the Sound towards Tebrat and rendezvous with the Ullapool lifeboat. They will make contact direct. Out."

"Wilco, coastguard, standing by."

Chapter 12

All three were back at Inverstack House by 6 pm. The handover of the rib to the lifeboat crew went smoothly and as soon as John's boat was on its trailer, they said au revoir and headed home. Duncan had been told by the lifeboat cox that the search for Jack would continue for a further two hours.

As they entered the house, Michelle said, "I'm for a shower. I want to get out of this wet dry suit."

"I think that goes for all of us," Derek echoed, going round to the rear of the Range Rover to take out the water-proof bag. Duncan's wet rope was now in the other one.

"I'll see if I can persuade my dear housekeeper to rustle up high tea, which is the greatest thing since Christ left Partick." Duncan gave a bellow of a laugh.

"Don't ask, Michelle. Christ was never in Partick, which in case you don't know, is a district of Glasgow." Duncan paused at the door of the house and looked back at Derek.

"Tell me, Mr Hawthorne," he grinned. "Since when did you have an interest in photographing kelp. Good God, man, I nearly burst out laughing."

"Ah," Derek replied with a smile. "I was wondering if you would notice."

"What the blazes is this double talk?" Michelle looked from one to the other.

"It was a particularly edible variety."

"Shit," Duncan responded, "you must be getting senile, but I have my suspicions."

"What a pair," Michelle muttered, shaking her wet hair. "You're like a couple of kids – insinuations and a private language."

"It will all come out in the wash, girl," Derek replied. "Perhaps even before dinner."

It didn't take long for them to freshen up. Michelle had raced to their room and went straight into the shower, still wearing her dry suit. She yelled to Derek, who had just entered.

"I get priority, Derek, as I've an injury." She gave her infectious laugh and unzipped, throwing her suit to the floor.

"You should know by now that you can leave your clothes on under the suit." He informed her.

"Ah," she responded, putting her head and a bare leg outside the door. "But it's more sensuous like this."

"Don't take all day, then, or I'll come in there and join you."

"Please."

"Where's your better half, Michelle?" Duncan quizzed when she entered the lounge. He hadn't yet got the fire going.

"I had first shot of the shower, but he's out and fiddling with his computer."

"Well, he'd better get his finger out or he'll miss the fresh scones. Mrs Mathieson has been busy as a fairy and will be emerging from the kitchen any minute, and she won't be pleased with me as she was preparing dinner. The holy of holies," he confided, "venison in red wine and her own rowanberry jelly."

"Yum," Michelle approved. "You have a hard life of it, Duncan, spoiled rotten."

"Talking of being spoiled" Duncan looked up for he had started the fire lighting ritual. "There are four other showers in the house and three baths, not counting the Victoriana special. The bath of a hundred jets."

"That I must try," she replied, breaking into song:

'I'm just an old-fashioned girl.
'I want an old-fashioned house, with an old-fashioned fence,
'And an old-fashioned millionaire...'

"Meantime – here's some more kindling."

Duncan roared with laughter, which was followed by an excited oscillation of four tea trolley castors on the wide hardwood floorboards. Mrs Mathieson appeared round a serious array of silverware, plum conserve, potato scones and butter from Andrew Martin's farm up the glen.

"I had Highland Radio on in the kitchen a few minutes ago and when I heard singing, I thought that the programme had changed to that request affair. What I did hear was that the chap's boat has been found, Mr MacGillvery. I remember him being here once."

"We found his boat, but not Jack. It doesn't look good, I'm afraid."

"Can you do the tea, Miss Michelle?" Her hand shook as she parked her trolley between the chairs.

"Of course," Michelle replied with concern. Mrs Mathieson gave a sniff and dabbed her eyes with a small silk handkerchief from residency in her left cuff.

"Dinner will be served at eight o'clock, sir," she announced with a degree of dignity as she retreated to her kitchen. Minutes later Derek entered. He had changed, now wearing a blue pullover and jeans. He was carrying his laptop and a package, which he put down on a chair and surveyed the goodies.

"I don't know if you appreciate it, MacGilivery," he greeted, "but you have a remarkable cook and baker in Mrs Mathieson."

"I can vouch for that, Derek," Michelle enthused, placing plum preserve on a potato scone.

"She is mentioned in my dispatches every night," Duncan agreed, looking at the revived fire.

"After I am re-fuelled and suitably preserved, I have something to show you," Derek promised.

"For goodness sake, eat up then," Michelle complained, securing a blob which was threatening to abandon her scone.

"Well," Derek announced some five minutes later. "Things are unfolding." He reached over to retrieve his computer from the chair with the other package. "When you thought I was losing my marbles recording the highlights of Laminariacae with my camera, in fact, that is what caught my eye initially, before something else – just above." He had his laptop open and a large close-up of kelp crowded the screen. "Now, study the following images, just above the kelp, on the rock wall."

"Good God, man," Duncan exploded, "bullet impacts."

"It's good to know that you have changed your mind about my mental state, Mr Laird." He continued. "There are ten cavities in the red sandstone caused by automatic fire and they all look remarkably fresh. Don't you agree, Duncan?"

"It takes me back to the Yemen, Derek, when a volley of 9mm rounds covered me in rock shards on similar rock, inches from my head."

"What does this mean?" Michelle cried out. "Not Jack?" Her cry ended in a sob.

"It looks sinister," Duncan said in a whisper.

"Also, when I went aboard Jack's rib I had a look in the waterproof locker in the console." He unwrapped the package and drew out some papers in a sealed plastic bag. "I haven't had a chance to look at these," he said, handing some to Duncan.

"Thanks."

Derek's lot comprised some of Jack's business cards and a diary containing various small drawings and figures, probably data from his harbour job.

"Anything of interest, Duncan?" he asked. "Nothing much here."

"I wasn't expecting a great deal," his friend replied. "Jack kept everything of importance between his ears. But there's a phone number on the back of a photo here of his house in Cumbria. It has his sister's name on it, followed by a Keswick exchange number. If I remember correctly, she lives there." He looked up, his face pensive. Just then the house phone rang. "Excuse me, it's probably the police or the coastguard." He went to the extension. "Duncan MacGilivery…

"It's Angus Beaton."

"What can I do for you Angus?"

"My son, Magnus, was searching the shore by the house today and he came across a damaged digital camera in the water. It appears as dead as the *Ark Royal* but I thought I would mention it. Could it belong to your friend, Jack Rippon?"

Duncan paused. "I know that Jack had a camera, but I can't recollect the model."

"It's a well worn Nikon – it looks as if the water has got inside."

"I have to be down your direction in the morning, Angus, and I could call by and pick it up." He continued, "If it is Jack's, I can have it passed on to his sister, but the police will have to see it first."

"That's fine, Duncan. Young Magnus will be excited if it turns out to be a clue. He told me that he was going to leave it on the shore as it was so mangled, but common sense prevailed."

"Thanks for phoning, Angus, see you tomorrow." He went back to the fire. Michelle was studying the bullet impact holes on the computer.

"I'll have a try tweaking them later, Derek."

"Something else has come up," Duncan announced. "That was the boatman from Tebrat. You met him, Derek. It transpires that his son, who was searching the shore at his house, found a beat up Nikon waterproof camera. I've just remembered that Jack had a Nikon for his work."

There was a silence, then a few crackles from the fire. Derek spoke. "That could possibly shed light on his fate, Duncan?"

"I wouldn't have any hopes if I were you. The camera is damaged and water has got in." He continued, "I'm collecting it tomorrow and perhaps we should have a good look at it before I pass it on to Superintendent Montgomery." He pondered for a moment and said, "I think that I had better go down on my own. It wouldn't be good to show too much interest. I did imply that I could send it on to his sister. In fact, we now have her telephone number."

Duncan told Michelle she could use the office computer

and the laser printer for Derek's pics. "I'll be back in a couple of hours," he added.

Again the weather was fine for the last day's search. The RAF team had come across diving mask, floating in a sea pool, below the Sanday cliffs, opposite the beach at Tebrat. They thought they could be of military origin, but couldn't be sure with so much surplus gear on the market.

Duncan drew up at the Beatons' white-washed cottage. It was set in an idyllic location with sea views across the Sound and in the distance he could see the mountains of the Outer Hebrides, with the Butt of Lewis looking like Ultima Thule, shrouded in a blue mist. Hens pecked the close cropped machair as if scratching for precious stones. A red-haired boy appeared at the doorway and gave a wave.

"Magnus, isn't it?" Duncan shouted. The big man walked over to him from his Range Rover. "Sunday, no school today, Magnus."

"Thank goodness, Mr MacGillvery. I like it much better here."

"So would I, young man. I'd never go away. Oh, hold on a minute. I've got something for you." He went back to the vehicle and came back with a bundle of magazines. "These are for you as you found the camera – *Modern Search and Rescue*." Magnus's face broke into a great smile.

"Thanks, sir. I think the camera is scrap, but I'll get it. Dad and Mum are out visiting an aunt who's unwell."

"You say that I'm asking for them." They walked over to the cottage. Magnus went ahead, clutching his new posses-sions, and came out in an instant, holding a co-op carrier bag.

"This is it, Mr MacGillvery, a bit of a mess, I'm afraid." Duncan didn't open the bag.

"Thanks, Magnus. I'm sorry that I've got to return as I have another call to make."

"Goodbye, sir."

Duncan drove off, feeling guilty at not spending more time with the lad.

Chapter 13

"I've something of interest, Derek," Duncan announced as he entered and handed him the carrier bag. "I haven't had a chance to look at it yet," he added. "Where's that woman of yours?"

"I like the way you refer to me as 'that woman', MacGillvery." Michelle was descending the stairs, holding some large prints.

"Just a figure of speech, Michelle," he laughed. "Let's go into my office."

They followed Duncan and Michelle put the enlargements on a polished oak table. The two men studied them briefly.

"These are pretty good, Michelle," Duncan observed.

"The usual from that woman," Derek smiled. "But for the moment, we had all better contribute to solving the problem in this co-op bag before salt water devours it." He removed the camera and placed it on the table. A dribble of water accompanied this operation.

"I think you had better take over, Michelle," he suggested. "You have the experience of underwater camera work with marine surveys."

"In fact, I have the identical model!" She confirmed. "Let me have a better look." She broke the waterproof seal on the flexible plastic casing. More brackish water ran out on to the carrier bag.

"Have you an old towel and a basin of warm water, Duncan?" She paused. "Also a fan heater."

"You sound like Mrs MacLeod, Michelle," he said as he moved to the door. "She's a retired mid-wife."

"That pal of yours, Derek, has missed his vocation."

By the time Duncan returned, she had the camera partly stripped. Derek had established the source of the leak. A bullet had gone through the outer plastic casing and must have severed the lug of the lanyard. Probably, the same bullet smashed the LCD screen.

"Here are the things you wanted, Michelle."

"Thanks, Duncan. Can you put the towel on the table top for the basin. The heater we will use later."

"Looks as if it took a direct hit, Duncan." He passed over the plastic casing. Duncan studied it. Michelle, who had just taken out the memory card, put it on the table top with slow deliberation. She looked confused.

"I was wondering why you had such an interest in this bit of plastic, Derek. Both of you seem to have an accept-ance of violent death. It follows you about; you are like magnets attracting bullets."

"It was our way of life, Michelle," he spoke kindly. "That was our job."

"It's silly of me." She gave a sniffle. "I know that Jack was a good friend and we all want to find out what happened." She lifted up the memory card. "This little chap may contain some information for us. It has plenty of capacity. It may be all right they're pretty robust. We can plug it into one of the computers." She continued, "On various marine projects in the Med we regularly get salt in electronic equipment. There, the salt concentration is about 38ppt – in case you don't know, that's particles per million. Now, first of all, I will give the camera a bath in Duncan's water, metaphorically speaking," she smiled, "and get rid of some of the eastern Atlantic salt.

"Derek, dry this card very gently, using these insulated forceps, once Duncan has kick started that medieval fan heater. It was probably made to put some poor punkah wallah out of business. I'll get my computer."

"That girl never ceases to amaze me, Derek," Duncan exclaimed when she left. "She should have been in our outfit."

"I suppose," Derek admitted, as he directed the heater, "we might have had a touch of humanity!"

"You're getting soft, you bugger." Duncan shook his head. In minutes, Michelle returned, clutching her laptop.

"I hope that you haven't overcooked it, Derek."

"Not a chance; you know my ability with a chip pan."

She took it from him and tested its temperature in the palm of her hand.

"Well, let's give it a go." She plugged it into her computer, but it didn't fire up so she tried to open it in the Lightroom programme. Nothing. Then she switched her computer off and on several times and the screen came to life.

"Those were a few tense moments," Duncan breathed.

In seconds they saw that there were eighteen pictures on file. She hit 'browse' and boxed images appeared. The first five or six were probably records of the moorings job he had been working on, the next was a good shot of the island of Sanday with the Great Stack in the foreground. There was silence in the room as three faces were entranced, for she had changed to full page frame. There was a gasp and Derek said,

"Hell's teeth."

The shot was obviously from inside the Great Stack at low water, for three stumpy legs protruded like enormous feet of an old armchair, revealing at least three arches, with their tops above the water. It must have been a wide angle shot for, to the right, a series of sloping ledges, like giant wide steps, led upwards out of the frame.

"So it's true about the stack being on legs with a huge chamber underneath." Derek, for once, looked excited.

"It's just as was described by Callum, the boatman all those years ago," Duncan added.

"Let's see the next one, Michelle," Derek said, "before I wet myself."

The next was a shot looking up the ledges. They seemed to rise at least thirty metres to the shadows of the roof, well above the top ledge or step. The flash wasn't sufficiently powerful to see any detail. But the lower steps were sharp and damp; they were obviously natural and comprised of angular chunks of red Torridonian sandstone of varying thicknesses. They also appeared to match the depth of the natural fault lines in the bedrock on the periphery of the image.

"This looks as if it was taken at low tide," Michelle observed.

"Exactly what I was thinking," Derek cut in.

"In which case we should be able to make an accurate guess – if there is such a thing – as to when the photograph was taken, once we get data on tide levels, of course," Duncan suggested.

"Could be," his pal agreed, "you being an accredited detective. Let's have the next pic, Michelle," Derek suggested. "Don't listen to this old fart. It's like being at a matinee when I was a kid."

"I'd like to have been an onlooker." Michelle smiled at her boyfriend.

Jack's next image appeared to have been taken higher up on the stairway. The steps were closer together and nature seemed to have been assisted, for these were now more defined as if they had been hewn from the rock. There was no clue as to how high above the water this was.

"It appears that Jack also found the difference in the step size significant," Michelle commented. "It's like a 'picture book' for a movie."

"Let us move on," Derek pleaded. "There are things ahead and we know not what they be."

"Who the heck wrote that?" Michelle, turned, an inquisitive light in her eyes. "Hannibal?"

"Colonel Derek Hawthorne, circa twenty-first century."

"I could have told you, Michelle," Duncan confirmed. "He can sound quite convincing sometimes."

"Don't I know it," she retorted.

All conversation ceased at the appearance of the next image. Michelle gave a gasp for, though she had seen the rapid sequence of pictures initially in the Lightroom programme, there had been no time to absorb their content, considering some were over exposed and the locations were unfamiliar. The current one was of the two final steps. In fact, above the top one was what appeared to be a blank, expansive area, which was poorly lit due to flash limitation. At the edge of this top step, the rim of the blank area, at a gap there was a wall possibly over a metre high. Just beyond this on the flat area was a short cutstone barrier. To gain access one would have to go round this obstacle. The wall was superb and built with interlocking blocks of red sandstone precise in their accuracy. It reminded her of Machu Picchu and the structural elements of the Inca ashlar wall.

"I don't think that I've seen workmanship like this since we chilled out in a Crusader castle in Jordan, Derek."

"Oh, I hear the tinkling of dishes." Duncan cocked his head to one side. That means Mrs Mathieson is on the dinner shift. She may take her wrath out on the gong any minute now which announces the ritual."

Michelle, bringing up the next picture, said, "Let's have a quick run through, a pre-dinner promo to chew over." These proved to be over-exposed. She continued in subdued tones as she expertly resurrected the files. "I think we have evidence of a major discovery, Derek. Doesn't it remind you of that cave you told me about, the Cosquer on the cliffs of the Calanques, where the entrance is thirty-seven metres under water?"

"It sure does. It was one of the major archaeological discoveries of the nineties. The charcoal paintings are unique. After it was discovered, it was then closed by the government for years to allow uninterrupted research."

"I checked on their prehistory report in the *Virtual Scientific Journal*," Michelle replied. "Our work back in Cambridge used on your wood sample was based on a similar carbon dating profile as was deployed there, the Tandetron method. It can be very accurate."

"In fact," Derek continued "Jack and I made one of the early dives there before it was closed. We heard about it from one of the French climbers who made the discovery."

"Jack may not have been out of his depth, so to speak, making this find inside the Great Stack," Duncan observed. Just then, the tintinnabulations of the gong spread its strident message.

As if by mutual agreement, over dinner no one took up the subject of the last few hours. That evening, Mrs Mathieson was driving the culinary machine from the kitchen and food was served by her sometimes kitchen help, Daisy Maybole, a plump, cheerful lady who wore elasticised stockings and had highly polished cheeks. After the meal they retired to the office with instructions to Daisy to serve coffee there in an hour. When they were back on their respective viewing chairs, Michelle fired her laptop as Derek spoke.

"Later, Michelle, can you transfer the stack files to a memory stick and delete your laptop copy. We can then work with one external source. In fact, I think it safer to format your computer hard drive and the camera memory as well."

Duncan cut in. "Yes, there are too many disagreeable things happening. Also, I'll have to hand Jack's camera to the police. Those files could raise awkward questions. But let's view the remainder before finally deciding."

Michelle commenced from where they left off. In minutes, she had readjusted the four images and they now transformed into reasonably sharp pictures. The group was silent as they absorbed the detail, trying to take in a myriad of shadows and highlights. The next pic of Jack's was of the door, which showed it to be to the left of the open area. This shot must have been taken beyond the baffle wall. The door was now ajar and it appeared to be of formidable construction, possibly cut from very thick slate, and it was reflecting light. Beyond this vault door was a large chamber hewn from the sandstone. There appeared to be dirty looking bundles on the floor which were difficult to identify. Their eyes automatically switched to the next picture to try to obtain clues as the illumination seemed infinitely better.

"It looks as if he used his diving lamp to get more light," Duncan said, breaking a silence which must have lasted several minutes.

"Those bundles are decayed wicker baskets, I think," Michelle murmured, enlarging one on the screen. "Yes, look," she cried out, "you can just see among the dust the sharp edges of pottery and metal. Derek, I have a feeling that your wood carving may have been the key to unlock that door."

It was difficult to establish what the heaps were composed of Michelle moved on and the next pic required even more tweaking, but at last they had a different angle of the floor, though it was still impossible to place things as there were further collections of similar piles with no way of relating them. To one side there was what looked like the remains of a box or chest, as decayed metal banding was leaning inwards, probably against the contents. Here, too, in the debris were pinholes of reflected light, probably from Jack's lamp.

"Can you bring up these tiny reflections, Michelle," Derek asked quietly.

"Sure."

"I think these are from cut gem stones," Duncan said, deliberating. "It's difficult to tell as these pics have been getting progressively darker. He probably had trouble getting back out if his inspection lamp was running down. I have a question for you both."

"Let's have it," Michelle prompted.

"Imagine yourselves in Jack's shoes – or fins – and you have just found Aladdin"s cave. What would be your instincts?"

"If it was me, I'd take a few sample trinkets back."

"I think that would go for me, too, otherwise it would be like reporting seeing yeti prints, but no yeti."

"Or, nearer home," Duncan added, "saying you saw the Loch Ness Monster, but had run out of film or battery power."

"The weight of Jack's samples would ensure he wouldn't float to the surface," Derek suggested.

Chapter 14

It was midnight before they decided to pack up. Michelle had finished formatting the hard discs and Jack's camera chip. The Nikon was now re-assembled ready for Duncan to take to Superintendent Montgomery in the morning.

They had a leisurely breakfast. Duncan brose with butter. Michelle a croissant and local honey, the former freshly made by the ubiquitous Mrs Mathieson, and Derek a high calorie fried egg platter of Lorne sausage, fried potato scones, chips, fried tomatoes, black pudding and mushrooms.

"I was thinking." Duncan spoke as he placed his empty wooden bowl on the dining table, "that we should have a plan of action." He looked at his two friends earnestly. "We seem to be caught up in some strange subterfuge. At least, I am for neither of you were involved in the explosion."

"Could they be linked?" Derek prompted.

"I'm not sure. but I have a gut feeling that they are. Its too much of a coincidence that this violence erupted – so to speak – with a land mine: result one fatality, nearly three. Then Jack riddled with automatic fire.

"I've been deliberating, too. Duncan." Derek cleaned his

platter with a circular flurry with his fork speared into a remnant of a potato scone. He swallowed this before continuing. "You're right: there must be a connection."

"There could be serious treasure in the stack." Michelle spoke quietly, looking at her two companions. "I should, perhaps, say, left in the Great Stack." She paused and realised that she had their attention. "I didn't think much of it at the time, but I did later, that there was a lot of wood debris lying about the floor. There was nothing beneath. I suspect a good proportion of the Templar loot has been taken!"

The two men looked at her and remained quiet. Derek was the first to comment. "I thought my power of observation was pretty good, but you have the ability to see what's not there: things which may have fallen to bits or buried beneath the floor of the sea. It's a salutary lesson."

"Yes, good thinking, girl. I feel doubly grieved," Duncan complained. "First, I'm nearly blown to bits and blinded and then Jack... Other than a sinister black rib and wreckage on Bealach Uiske we have nothing to go on. I'll help you to recover the remains of the Crusader loot, Derek. It may give us a lead."

"Whoever they are, they want to remain incognito," Derek stated, "and they don't appear to care who gets in the way."

"What about the police, Duncan?" She looked up.

"In connection with the explosion, that's in the hands of Special Branch and the M–something – I am not sure of the second bunch who interviewed me. I don't think they will be requesting assistance from the local constabulary. I will do my duty and give a statement about our part in the search and you two and John may have to provide an account of the recovery of the rib. I will also identify Jack's camera, which still has some water in it."

"You're a cunning sod." Michelle couldn't resist a laugh.

"Perhaps you now realise, Michelle, our precaution in wiping your hard drive and the camera."

"I haven't been knocking about with you, Colonel, without realising that a spade's not a spade, but a burial implement."

The phone rang, then stopped. Mrs Mathieson came into the room.

"It's for you, Mr Duncan. Dr Bell."

"Excuse me for a moment." Duncan went out to the hall. "Hello, David, checking on your patient?"

"I heard that you had taken up boating, so I assumed that you were still with us and can see. However," he added, "I'd better call and give you the once over or John Black will be reporting me."

"I'll be here this afternoon if that suits. About three."

"That's fine. It's my day off."

"See you, David."

When Duncan returned to the dining room he told his two friends that he was off to the local police headquarters. "It's a super morning. I think I'll walk. Incidentally, that was Dr David Bell on the phone. He's the chap I shared the landmine with. He heard that I was out boating."

"How much does he know, Duncan?"

"Just what I told you, Derek. He knows nothing about the treasure. He'll be here at 3 pm."

"There was another point about the grotto." It was Michelle. "Like me, you probably wondered about the lack of prints on the floor. I double checked the images and it's possible that any evidence of disturbance could have been obliterated by damp or condensation. There seemed to be a reflection off the floor."

"It doesn't add up," Duncan pondered, leaving the table.

"I think a visit to the stack is overdue." He looked at Derek. "It's about time that you made a list of requirements. You know what we need, you have the contacts."

Duncan strode along the drive to the main road. The snow had almost vanished with the early spring. The sun slanted down with confident heat. He noticed that the great boles of the sequoias were encircled with snowdrops, their pristine white heads and lithe stalks reminding him of young nuns in a Dolomitic convent years ago. He recalled that his thought at the time was, what a waste. Dave was with him on that trip and as well as being a great companion, he was fluent in both Russian and German. As he strode down the road, he passed the time of day with various locals, some giving him a longer look than normal – his face still had an albino quality.

Superintendent John Montgomery stood up from behind his desk as Duncan entered. The policeman seemed fit, though he had given up running some time ago. He held out a hand over the desk to greet his friend, speaking in a broad Highland accent.

"It's good to see you, Duncan. We thought you were a goner, but I see you'll have to get some eyebrow pencil – ad interim, of course."

"I'm feeling fine again, John. Dave is coming round this afternoon so, hopefully, I'll get a clean bill of health." He sat down opposite the policeman, who was about to ask for two cups of coffee over the intercom. "Not for me, thanks." Duncan held up his hand. "I had a late breakfast." He continued, "Any news regarding the search?"

"Not a thing. It's a strange business. We're winding things up this evening."

Duncan took Jack's camera from his pocket and put in on the desk.

"It was his, all right. I know, from its waterproof pouch, but the salt water got at it and it drowned. I can give you his sister's number; she's in Keswick. But I haven't contacted her as I was waiting for the conclusion of the search."

"The coastguard think that he couldn't survive this long, even with a dry suit. He was a professional diver, I gather." He looked quizzically at Duncan.

"Yes. He got bored in civvie street and chose jobs he fancied. He has called in to see me several times, or I would meet up with him. We were in the army together."

"What we find baffling is why that elaborate mooring of the boat." The superintendent looked puzzled and studied Duncan carefully. The big man wore his sphinx face.

"We couldn't understand that either. That geo isn't shown on the charts. The only thing we could think of was that he was hoping to get a couple of big lobsters just off the cliffs and at the time the sea was too rough and too deep to anchor his rib." Duncan added, "He always turned up with a succulent crustacean for dinner."

"Seems to me a lot of trouble for a lobster." The police-man didn't sound convinced.

Duncan smiled, recalling that John came from a long line of fishermen. "I'll give you a statement if you require one, John. The same goes for my two friends and John Lightfoot, I'm sure."

"I'll have a word with the fiscal and let you know."

"Oh, I almost forgot." He produced a piece of paper and handed it to the superintendent. "That's the number of Jack's sister."

"Thanks."

Duncan rose, but paused. "What is the outcome of the Bealach Uiske explosion?"

"You know probably better than me, once the military

and Special Services enter the frame, they take over." He added, "I gather that your friend had a history before he retired – Special Commendation, Military Medal and all that – even his rib is ex-military. The coastguard spotted that right away. It does seem a bit odd after such an illustrious career." John Montgomery arched his eyebrows and looked down at his desk. "Don't you think so?"

"I have no answer to that, John. I didn't see him but I do know he was a master of that watery underworld; that's why he was in SBS. I would like to find out for myself."

"Well, I can only hope that you keep me informed, Duncan. The force has respect for your ability, but I expect it will be another case of Death by Misadventure. We have had about six such incidents this year; it's the popularity of sea kayaking and amateur diving."

Dr Bell caught up with Duncan in his car just as he was approaching the house.

"You're walking all right," David greeted him from the open window. Duncan opened the passenger door.

"Hello, Dave. I've been seeing John Montgomery."

"At first sight, you don't look as if you are going to die from your wounds," he said as they got out of his car at the house.

At the entrance, David paused. "Hold on, I've got something to show you. It's in the boot." He came back with his attaché case of medical gear and also a small package.

"I thought it might be a bottle of malt, Dave, but the shape isn't right."

"Correct. Much more interesting!"

Derek was in the lounge with Michelle. Both were using laptops.

"Dave, this is Michelle, a marine archaeologist and the resident brains. You have met Derek before."

"Hi, doc, good to see you again. I gather that you had a narrow squeak, too."

"It wasn't too bad," the doctor confessed, though I couldn't play my pipes for a few days."

"A blessing," Duncan muttered quietly. "You'll have to excuse us. David has to work out why I'm still alive. We'll go into my study, doc."

"We'll have a chat later," Michelle chimed in.

It took twenty minutes for David to establish that his friend was in rude health, as he used to say, and he quickly returned his tools of trade back to their case.

"You're firing on all cylinders, Duncan, and you can return to your merry band of rescuers."

"That's a relief," Duncan replied, pulling on his shirt and fleece. "I haven't got time to laze about."

"I had a memo from Dr Black about the analysis of the explosive dust taken from your skin, Duncan. You are probably familiar with various explosive devices. Black is pretty tidy about such things and he's reasonably sure it could be a M16A2 USA, 600G land mine, a powerful beast. He was a bit worried about the explosive charge."

"My personal opinion," Duncan replied, "is that it was bloody effective."

"Let's join the others for the important aspect of this visit," David announced. They moved next door.

"Hi, you two," Duncan greeted. "I'm still alive and doc has something to show us." They looked up.

"This is my offering," David announced, unwrapping the package. "What do you think?"

"Hell's bells, where did you get it?"

Derek took it gingerly from David and went to the

window to have a better look. "Good God, where did it come from?"

Duncan and Michelle came over and studied the ornamental cap or jug lid, obviously of gold, with what looked like diamonds studded at intervals round the perimeter. It was spectacular and the metalwork of the rim was intricate.

"I found it yesterday, or rather, re-discovered it. I was going to take my anorak with me which I haven't had on since the explosion." He then told them of finding the cap in the snow and stuffing it in a pocket. "It was only after coming across it that I remembered the incident. Not uncommon in the circumstances."

"Michelle is an expert in medieval things," Duncan stated. "What do you think, lass?"

"But where did this come from. It surely wasn't lying in the snow?" she said, studying it closely. "Without a detailed examination, I can't positively identify it, but my guess is that it's a stopper or cap of an ornamental beaker, possibly medieval Saracen. The workmanship is exceptional and it is valuable. Also, I would think that the gold content is well over 10 per cent and definitely over 300 years old." She looked up at the doctor, her eyes sparkling with excitement. "This qualifies it as treasure under the Treasure Act of 1966, that is in England and it should be sent for dating and evaluation. I could send it to colleagues who are expert in this period first and they could forward it on to the Museums of Scotland."

"Well, well," Duncan exclaimed, sitting down. "You never know what to expect in a blizzard, other than frostbite and burns. What do you think, Derek?"

"I would put it down to coincidence."

Duncan knew that this was a fib.

"Our lab in Cambridge, David, has an Electron

Microscopy Suite and it would be possible to get a proper analysis of the metal. I have contacts there and could approach them on your behalf. It would be more expedient if I sent it to them. It would be all legal and above board."

"Sounds good," the doctor agreed.

"It's a bit of a mystery how it got to one of the most remote parts of the Scottish Highlands," Michelle said, mystified.

"A pity you didn't come across the parent beaker," Derek said.

"I don't think that there is much point in searching Bealach Uiske," Duncan ventured. "If there was an ancient beaker there when we were almost blown to bits, I'm sure it won't be there now. The Crash Recovery Squad never misses anything. It'll have taken up residence in Farnborough!"

Chapter 15

Dr David, who intended to get some exercise on this his day off, departed, promising to see them soon. The others didn't say anything for some minutes after he left. The three of them went back to the lounge.

"I was about to suggest that there could be some connection with the stack find, but I managed to hold myself in check," Michelle stated, looking from Derek to Duncan. "I assume David knows nothing about it?"

"That's correct," Duncan volunteered. "I would certainly like it to remain that way, for I don't want him to get involved."

"Exactly my sentiments," Derek agreed. "This brings up another aspect; your role in all this, Michelle. What started as an innocent hobby has developed into a dangerous situation. I would drop the whole thing if it wasn't for Jack, but we owe him one."

"Don't worry about me. I'm just not so brave as you guys; I'll keep out of range."

"Derek's right, Michelle." Duncan was deadly serious. "There are some nasty people out there."

"Tell me," Duncan asked her. "What's the low-down on David's oriental stopper?"

"I'm fairly sure it belongs to the period pertinent to the Order, but of course I will get a better idea once the museum checks it, but new regulations decree that it will have to be sent to Scotland now for evaluation. It is a rare piece of wonderful craftsmanship. But how did it get there?" She looked at Duncan perplexed. But it was Derek who replied.

"I think that the explosion has a direct connection with the stack treasure and probably the contents of those missing piles – the mounds which are now just dust were on that aircraft."

"If your hypothesis is right, our Bealach plane, which, incidentally, was an Islander, may have crashed with the artefacts on board, destined for some overseas market." Duncan looked thoughtful and continued, "In which case the helicopter Doc and I saw from the climb could have been on a salvage mission, hence the overkill, using that obviously powerful land mine to destroy evidence, after, of course, they had recovered the loot."

"Wouldn't that suggest some operator with a base on the west coast of Scotland?" Michelle put forward.

"Possibly." Derek looked thoughtful.

"It certainly raises the stakes. It means whoever is behind it has considerable resources for a light aircraft was sacrificed – and possibly a pilot," Michelle suggested.

"I think that you have something there." Duncan rubbed an irritating eyebrow. "The only strange report has been that big rib. That, too, must have a home." He had a sudden thought. "The coastguard chopper will be over here for a rescue team communication briefing at the weekend and the pilot is a friend. I'll speak with him this evening to give him time to ask the crews if they have spotted our mystery chopper or a large black rib, which must leave a distinctive wake."

"There are several other possibilities," Derek pontificated. "I think, Michelle, that you could consult Google, their satellite mapping info. It may be a long shot, which could possibly show some maritime surface activity or even aircraft. You know the co-ordinates. Also, another task when you are at the keyboard, to keep an eye on international website auctions for rare medieval artefacts – you know what to check out. It's unlikely so soon, but you never know."

"And your task in all this, master mind?" she replied in mock subservience.

"I have much pending, which I will divulge in a minute, but regarding the aspect under discussion, surveillance, I will contact my US partners in crime and will also get some satellite images, 'Day and Night', and go over them with a fine tooth comb. Also, you, Duncan, are aware that there are lots of Big Brothers watching from the heavens with all the nuclear submarine activity in this part of the world, playing their war games. There are many new toys if I can just access them, such as SAR, Synthetic Aperture Radar, etc."

"Next?" Michelle prompted.

"Well, it's not your remit, but Duncan will appreciate it."

"Oh?"

"Yes, I managed to locate all the items on my shopping list and they will arrive soon, including the hire of a cargo rib, a big bugger of eleven metres, with four, two-fifty horse motors. You know," he continued "Scotland must be one of the best places in the world for hiring such boats. They are as common as seagull shit in Aberdeen. Well, not quite," he admitted. "That brings up another thing, Duncan."

"Oh?"

"We need a base to hide this beast, for it will stand out like a sore thumb. A private harbour or something of that ilk."

"Right, I'll put it on my agenda," his friend replied. "And thinking about spies in the sky, I just remembered something, a bit of light relief." Duncan gave a wide grin. "A sputnik crashed near here some years ago, nobody seems to know much about it. It was probably one of the early ones – some had a monkey or a dog strapped inside for experiments. It was found by a team member searching for a missing bomber. It was less than two metres in diameter and had been stripped of all contents, also, I presume, its rhesus passenger. The only items located, some distance away, were plastic containers with clear liquid inside."

"What a weird story," Michelle marvelled. "I wonder, MacGillvery, if your tales are true or are you exercising a vivid imagination?"

"It is strange," Duncan agreed, "and what's more weird is that the removal of the contents was professionally done."

"Could it have been dismantled by a Russian team?" Derek suggested.

"My own thoughts, Derek, for at that time, at the height of the Cold War, there were numerous so-called Russian trawlers monitoring these waters and possibly when a high profile satellite crash landed, a stealth squad from a trawler could have been dropped off to collect the bits. Interesting?"

"Very," Derek responded. "Nothing has changed."

"I'd better get David's 'cap' off to the museum. Duncan, can I wrap it up in the office?"

"Sure, you'll find all the necessaries in the cupboard behind my desk." Michelle went out with David's package.

"Thanks."

"Derek, I have had a thought about a garage for your new toy."

"Well?" his friend replied. "Shoot."

"I don't know if you recall seeing buildings several miles beyond the geo, on the other side of the Sound. They are in a little bay facing north and it was an old boatyard. It went bankrupt some four years ago. It has since reverted to the estate, neighbours of mine and they own the property."

"Sounds interesting." Derek looked up, all attention.

"It's locked up at present but has power and is ready for a fresh tenant, but I doubt if it will ever be used again. There's no market for new fishing boats these days; they are all being scrapped due to the new European Commission rulings."

"Sounds ideal. Can we get the use of it?"

"I'm sure. I can give him a ring. He's abroad for a few weeks, visiting his son."

"That's super if you can do that. I will arrange the delivery there if it's OK. While you're at it, can you order 4,000 litres of fuel – I presume there's a road?"

"Yes, a single track. It's about four kilometres from a B junction. I'll show you on the map. There's a jetty adjacent to the slip. If a boat is at the top of the slip or at the jetty, it's undercover. There's a very large roller door and it has the remoteness of a Tibetan gompa."

"You haven't questioned the rib size, Duncan."

"No. I know you have your reasons" He studied his friend. He never doubted Derek's ability at applying his mind to a problem and working out the solution. He was like Jack in many ways, a combination of ruthlessness and logic, and, he added to himself, ability.

"Well, it's big enough to outpace the black one, which may be important and has enough room to accommodate the contents of the stack's strong room in one go. There are other things, too, such as a submersible, inflatable raft on top of which a small inflatable dinghy can attach so that we can tow it and its underwater contents on the raft without attracting suspicion. This will probably only be of use for getting clear of the stack under the archway, for there's plenty of space in the rib for a large cargo, 6,000 kg in fact. Also, I acquired with some difficulty an array of self-defence items."

"I was wondering about that," Duncan said slowly. "I thought I might have to dig out my 12 bore and deer rifle." He looked at his friend with a serious frown. "I don't want to crap on my own doorstep, Derek. Everything has to be discreet – just like the old days." Just then Michelle came in. "I'm going down to the post office, Derek, before it closes. Do you want to stir yourself?"

"Yes, I could do with giving my eyes a rest."

"Duncan?"

"Much as I enjoy your company, that man of yours has ordered me to make phone calls."

Michelle received coveted glances as she walked down to Glen Dhu post office. They presented an interesting couple, Derek some thirty centimetres taller, his coppery hair contrasting with Michelle's blonde.

One old lady confided in her companion, somewhat her senior and obviously hard of hearing and with the power of a public address system bellowed: "No, Flora, I don't think he's her bodyguard. You have been watching too many of those American soaps," and added to Flora, "You know, the reason that they are called soaps is that they need cleaning up; that's what the minister told me the other day."

It was about 6 pm before they gathered in the lounge. There were notes to compare and a late tea was waiting expectantly on Mrs Mathieson's trolley. Duncan was perched on a sofa, with Michelle and Derek opposite on armchairs. Michelle volunteered as self-appointed tea dispenser.

"I have positive news on two phone calls," announced Duncan. There was almost a trace of smugness in his voice. He paused.

"Well, are you going to spit it out, or do I have to wring it out of you?" Derek encouraged. "Ah, thanks, Michelle." He interrupted the badgering and took a cup of Darjeeling.

"Patience was never your strong point, Hawthorne." Duncan always used his friend's surname when he wanted to rebuke him. "First, I spoke with the SAR chopper OC and he gave me some heavy info, even without having to consult his crews. All interesting sightings are logged as they have cameras on board. He told me that he had seen a Eurocopter flying west across the Minch in the direction of Harris at dusk, when he was returning from a maritime call-out."

"When was this?"

"About a month ago. He will let me know."

"Any identification?"

"No. It was getting dark. In respect of large, inflatable ribs, he told me that there are quite a few. They are used widely for sport fishing and for taking tourists sightseeing. For example, there are regular trips to St Kilda and other islands."

"Your pal who has the boatyard?"

"All arranged. I had to think of a plausible reason for wanting the place, then I thought of the Manx Shearwater."

"That sounds like a round the Isle of Man power boat race," Derek suggested.

"Good guess, but it's a bird, a nocturnal bird. Puffinus puffinus, a native of the west coast of Scotland which lives in burrows. It will give us good cover for working at night."

"It's a great idea, Duncan, perfect. Other than poaching, I can't think of a better excuse for Witching Hour excursions. How about a banner for the rib with 'MANX SHEARWATER SURVEY' emblazoned on it which we can attach to the side should the need arise."

"What's this about banners?" Michelle, who had just entered, asked. "You guys holding out on me?"

"Derek is about to take up boat building in his retirement," Duncan suggested, trying to look serious. "He'll tell you about it later. Before I was interrupted," Duncan said, "we collect the keys of the old boatyard from the factor and go out there to inspect it in the morning. Oh," he added, "fuel will be delivered if we find the place suitable."

Derek cut in. "You missed some of this, Michelle. Duncan may have got us a bolt hole for the rib. It's a disused boatyard."

"If the boatyard suits," Derek continued, "we will be able to take delivery of the rib immediately. We don't want to bugger about."

"Well, my contribution today has been paltry," Michelle confessed. "I stuck some stamps on the delectable beaker stopper parcel; even then Derek was lending a hand. But I did find time to search satellite images of the area and came across about half a dozen ribs. Not much of interest, I'm afraid. I saw mostly sick looking passengers wearing wet suits." She shuffled some papers, then continued. "However, there was one at," she consulted her notes, "taken at 18.10 hours. I have a date and references. This shows a large rib with three people on board in a high sea. Here is a print, not very good, I'm afraid, but the best I could download." She handed them an enlargement. Both men studied it carefully, Duncan looking over Derek's shoulder. It showed, unclearly, a boat, a large rib, with waves breaking over the bow; the outboards were just visible. The craft was as dark as the sea.

"It was a miracle that you spotted this, Michelle."

"I'm used to searching for minutia in my job, Duncan. That's how I found Derek." They all laughed.

"I am going to deploy a further slave to do my monitoring work," Derek announced. He addressed Michelle, who, unladylike, stuck out her tongue.

"First of all, Duncan, you may remember Bill Whiteman, who ran Surveillance night vision gear?"

"I certainly do, quite a whiz kid."

"Exactly. He left the Unit before we did and started a civvie security business specialising in image intensifier and infra-red gear. He's big time now, both here and in the US and is lending me the latest modified Sony HDS camera with an Astrascope Pro adapter, if you want all that crap, which can transmit images to a remote Control Software module which we can set up in here or wherever. The camera will enjoy views twenty-four hours a day on the cliffs across the Sound from the stack. If you need any more boring facts and figures... I'm sounding more like a salesman every day."

Duncan gave a moan. "At least I stick to natural history, not all this digital nonsense."

"You will eat your words, MacGillvery," Derek grinned.

"I think it's a great idea," Michelle chimed in. "Better than sitting on my behind on wet grass with binoculars for company."

"I'm glad you approve." He gave her an affectionate pat on the behind. "For you, my dear, will have to operate it." But, he added, "it comes with a satellite recorder so you can watch it when having a protracted shower. I should add that this bit of kit is classified and only available for real soldiers. Don't tell your dad about it. You know, Duncan.

Bill never misses a trick. He knew there was something of interest brewing and wanted to join in."

"I'm glad that he's not getting senile like some of us," was the reply.

"To change the subject, do you have a quad bike and trailer?"

"I have three and several trailers – our deer stalking clients are getting lazy."

"I must give you another of my instant quotes, Michelle," Derek stated.

'You can't accelerate the particles of time,
Unless you shake the hour glass.'

We have to get cracking!"

Chapter 16

David Bell started his hike to the north of the village. He was making the most of the late afternoon sunshine and admired the advent of early spring, though the snow had retreated to white fingers in the security of gullies where their steep sides, if you had a vivid imagination, could pass as scabbards. He felt a twinge in his fingers which reminded him that such innocuous scenes could change at these latitudes with dire consequences.

He took one last look at the escarpments ahead, for he was going to return to the village by the same route, when the strident notes of a pibroch emanated from his anorak pocket. His mobile was telling him he was wanted.

It was a call-out, not to the mountains, but to Harris where a diver was suffering from bends. The call was from the Maritime Rescue Co-ordination Centre at Lossiemouth. Apparently, both coastguard SAR helicopters based in Stornoway were deployed on an Atlantic emergency and a Merlin from the Co-ordination Centre, was now scheduled to transport the diver to the Marine Centre in Oban, on the mainland, which has a hyperbaric unit. The machine had to fly from the east coast of Scotland to the Outer Hebrides, picking up David en route at the small helipad at Glen Dhu. There was no other experienced doctor available.

He rang his practice and asked his secretary to arrange a locum to take over, a regular routine during call-outs. He didn't inform Duncan as he knew that he was up to his singed eyebrows with other problems.

Dusk was falling as they circled to land at a small airstrip in North Harris, a place new to David – and the pilot. An almost luminous deep red sun was dropping out of sight beyond the Island of St Kilda and from their elevated position, its rocky profile looked surreal with the twin fangs of Boreray and Stac an Armin rising almost 300 metres from a blood-coloured sea. Close by, the lights of the estate house stabbed the darkening scene as the machine hesitantly put down. The aircraft's landing lights were on and close to the doors of a large shed there was a parked pick-up truck and David, from the fuselage door, could see a man whom he took to be his patient, with a sleeping bag round his shoulders. He was lying in the rear. Two or three others were nearby, several, like the casualty, were wearing dry suits. Before they landed, David had discussed with the pilot over the intercom the procedure for the evacuation, for he wanted to diagnose the victim thoroughly before taking off, as decompression sickness comes in various forms. Also the flight to Oban was long and he didn't want to find that he had a case of tension pneumothorax to contend with without some prior knowledge. David and the winch man, who was carrying the oxygen, ran over to the vehicle as soon as the chopper's engines died.

A tall, thin man detached himself from the group and introduced himself. He had an accent which David recognised immediately, for he had spent some time in the Urals when he was a post graduate student.

"I am in charge here." His English was excellent. "This man," he swept his hand forward as he turned towards the vehicle, "is my employee and he was working on a shipwreck when he got into trouble. I think his condition is serious," he continued. "You are a doctor?"

"Yes, Dr David Bell, and you are?"

"Eugene Banderoski. I am in charge of the salvage operation at present working on a galleon." He went on, "The diver was at forty five metres and stayed down too long."

He then spoke to the workmen in Russian and they made room for the doctor to check the patient. David immediately administered oxygen. For some reason which he couldn't explain, he questioned the diver in English, even though the man's ability to communicate was limited.

"Perhaps I can help," Eugene offered, "he seems disorientated."

"Thanks." David took a torch from his rucksack and switched it on. As he turned, he put his rucksack on the tailgate and the beam caught the reflection of two large floodlights above the door of the building.

"Can you switch those lights on?" David swung the beam to the reflectors. "It will make things easier."

"Certainly," Eugene agreed. He called in Russian, "Igor, open up the side door and switch one floodlight on. Keep the doors closed, careful." Initially, David was surprised; there was something about the wording and tone of voice which was more of a warning than a request. He was suddenly wary and was conscious of a tension. He was about to continue with his examination but, subconsciously, looked up as the worker in a black anorak entered the side door and the doctor got a glimpse inside as an interior light was switched on. It seemed only a millisecond before the door was slammed closed and a spread of light flooded the area. However, in those brief moments reflected on a sheet of steel or glass propped against the inside wall he saw the distorted profile of part of a helicopter.

It was so brief that he thought at first that he had imagined it, but he knew it was for real.

"Ah, that's much better, many thanks," David said. It didn't take him long to realise that the diver was in a serious condition and suspected that he had also serious decompression illness likely cerebral, where the victim can suffer seizures and unconsciousness.

"Ewan, can you tell your boss on your RT that we will have to get this diver to the Hyperbaric Centre post haste. He's critical."

Before they could get the man on to the stretcher which was in the back of the vehicle, the Merlin had fired up. Eugene came over to the diver and spoke in Russian.

"You remember, Ivan, keep control, and don't answer any questions about your work." Eugene spoke to the doctor as they headed for the aircraft "Do you think he will survive, doctor?"

"I certainly hope so, he's going to a first class unit." He paused, "If we get there in time."

The following morning Duncan went to collect the keys of the boatyard from the factor's office in the village. He was away for the day, but his secretary had them ready on her desk. Derek and Michelle were waiting in the 4 x 4.

"Right, first stop the boatyard," Duncan announced as he got behind the wheel.

"This is exciting," Michelle exclaimed.

"I think, perhaps, dangerous would be a more apt

description," Duncan suggested, swivelling the sun visor for the low light was dazzling. He continued, "Did you get all your e-mails off, Derek?"

"Yes, There should be a bunch of replies when we get back."

It only took half an hour to reach the building. The single track dirt road was in good condition and they could see no obstacle which would impede the overgrown rib's delivery. They parked close to the main doors. The structure was constructed of breeze blocks and timber and to one side of the parking area there was a small empty cottage with boarded up windows.

"I could live in this area," Michelle shouted as she ran to the side of the main building, where the slip reached into the greenish blue sea. "This is super."

Derek joined her. "It sure looks ideal for our purpose," he agreed. "Perfect, in fact."

There was a rumbling noise and they realised that Duncan had gone inside, and switched on the power to operate the two main seaward doors. These opened upwards on rollers and were stowed in the spanning cross beam above the opening. They both moved round the edge of the slip into the building. Duncan was at the top of the ramp, holding the suspended control unit.

"Hey, you guys," he called. "Quite a place, don't you think, young man?"

"Sure is," Derek acknowledged. "Michelle is thinking of putting in an offer."

"It's tremendous, Duncan. Seriously, all that's missing are Vikings heading north in their long boats – didn't Hakon, the Viking King, pass by after his defeat at the Battle of Largs?"

"Yes," Duncan answered, "but he was probably dead

from his wounds by then. To answer your first question: I don't think Torkil MacKenzie-Baron would sell. Disposing of land is akin to an amputation of their private parts to some lairds."

"Well, that's a bit strong and I'm sure if anyone ever suggested that to Derek, he would think it a joke."

"I always take such matters seriously, Michelle, even from the most unlikely people."

"I'm sorry that I brought the matter up," Duncan confessed. "I think it may be better to consider the business in hand as this conversation could become personal, as politicians say; this place is 'fit for purpose', ideal for that flatulent craft of yours and it gets five stars for both remoteness and panoramic seascape. Have you worked out where you're putting the camera?"

"Just round the south headland according to this map." Derek pointed, "probably less than a kilometre away in a suitable hole in the rocks which should also give a hidey-hole for the dish. It should be at Inverstack tomorrow. Also, if I phone in the GPS info of the boatyard to the rib delivery driver, that, too, should be here tomorrow. They drive only at night."

"Hawthorne, both you and Duncan are like clones, with expressions of benign contemplation on your Kevlar faces, but behind the façade are scheming infernos where everything demands instant action."

"You've got to be a step ahead up the ladder, Michelle."

"Let's go round the headland and see if we can find a temporary home for Bill Whiteman's camera," Derek suggested and paused, "before I think of something else to say."

Michelle agreed. "Great idea, I love this place."

"I presume you have already thought about it, Derek, but our friend Bill will be able to monitor the camera as well as us. I know from bitter experience on a night raid, with a helmet cam. all the brass at Base were watching."

"Oh, yes, Duncan. I have a small caption arranged. It's a sketch of a clapper board in the form of a guillotine. He'll get the message."

"It's gratifying to note that you still have a semblance of humour despite your poker face," Michelle observed sweetly. A herd of red deer surveyed them from a hillock and they looked in surprisingly good condition considering the hard winter. On their left Sanday came into view. The sound wasn't flat calm today and a few white horses swept across the green sea. The Great Stack blended as usual with its parent island as if it was shy or perhaps embarrassed by its obesity. Though a few kilometres distant, Michelle was the first to spot a dark dot on the cliffs which was the geo.

"Can you see the cave, the geo?" She pointed.

"Just," It was Duncan. "I think the tide must be in for the entrance is barely visible.

"As I said, I had a look at the map," Derek stated. "I think the best spot for the camera is straight ahead, at a cliff top outcrop. It's about fifty metres above the sea." He was ahead of the other two and made a detour round a boggy section. "This is where the quad will come in handy, Duncan. Though the camera and powered pan head are only a few kilos, the lithium-ion battery is heavier."

"I've changed my mind – Good thinking, borrowing the camera gear, Derek, I can see us making use of it. As you suggested, Michelle can play her part from the shower and alert us if that black rib heads towards the stack when we are busy inside."

"My thoughts, too, Mr MacGillvery," Derek returned.

"At least I may be of some use at the sharp end, for I'll be able to monitor the Sound from the comfort of your 4 x 4 inside the boatyard, Duncan, which will be more comfort-able than the shower."

"Good idea," he replied approvingly. "It also has a trans-ceiver so we can keep in touch if absolutely necessary."

"Remind me to put a small vibration detector part way along the track, Michelle. We don't want you to be disturbed unawares."

"I'm reassured that you look after my welfare, Derek." She said demurely.

The rocky headland proved an excellent choice and just below the rim, beneath an overhang of rock, was a superbly hidden ledge completely invisible from above. Furthermore, several cracks on the edge of the escarpment could accom-modate the satellite antenna, depending on the angle requirements.

Chapter 17

It was after midnight before the Merlin returned to Glen Dhu helipad. There were not many facilities, a cat marking its territory squirting against a tree with unerring accuracy, a few house lights still on. In the darkened houses David thought there would be those awakened and muttering about idiots lost in the hills and the rest, the up-late birds, grateful that they hadn't gone to bed early.

The pilot spoke over the intercom. "Thanks for helping, David. At least we got him to the Unit in one piece."

"It was touch and go," the doctor replied. "Have a good trip back to Base." He remembered to take off his intercom lead before jumping on to the grass.

The machine rose above the village, the pilot dipped the nose and the floodlight in acknowledgement and climbed into a star-studded sky. The aircraft lights went out as he switched to NVG; only the tail strobe blinked.

David started the car, but didn't drive back home immediately. He just sat, reshuffling events. He realised that he hadn't yet fully recovered from the explosion. Even the short hike behind Glen Dhu had verified this and he mused, with a smile, on Duncan's medical: he was as fit as the proverbial flea, though there, he concluded, comparisons ended. Then, there was the landing on Harris. There was something fundamentally wrong, and the strange behaviour of Banderoski was odd, most odd, he told himself. He was obviously an intelligent scientist, yet he spoke openly in Russian to his men, one of whom switched on the floodlight. In this day and age Russian is used widely. He concluded that Eugene's stay in the Outer Isles, amongst a population of largely Gaelic speakers had given him a false sense of security. David was a believer in first impressions and warning bells pealed when he first spoke to the Russian. Was there any identification? A number on that helicopter, he was pretty sure there wasn't. Colour? That, again, was strange, a whitish grey, an anonymous colour. Duncan, he reflected, wouldn't be very happy with that bit of observation. Then, there were the people with Igor, shaven heads. Probably quite normal in the diving fraternity, yet they looked ex-military. Had Jack drowned ....? Drowning has a finality about it, a convenience; the sea claims one of its own, the sort of demise one expects from someone who has spent his life twiddling with mines. Jack hadn't been put to bed, so to speak, by his two friends. He seemed to be a presence like a back projection or perhaps conscience.

He put the car in gear and slowly made his way home. The moon had pulled itself over a serrated ridge, flooding the glen in a silver wash and the highlights in the Dhu, the Black River, below the road glinted like lazy mercury.

It was early afternoon when Duncan's Range Rover pulled up outside Inverstack. Michelle and Derek went to their room to collect their computers. Duncan retired to the office to check his mail. He was muttering to himself after having opened a tax demand when the phone rang.

"This is David."

"I'm still alive and kicking doc, or is it something else?"

"It is. I'm getting as paranoid as you."

"Call on me, anytime, Dave, you know that."

"I'll come over now, before surgery."

Twenty minutes later he heard David's voice in the lounge. He was speaking with Derek. The laird went through. "Come into the office, David. You had better join us, Colonel Hawthorne, unless the doctor has called to tell me that I have the clap."

"A different affliction, Duncan."

David propped himself on the edge of the desk. The other two remained standing. The doctor opened the conversation. "Since I last saw you I have been over to Harris on a diving emergency – bends. You may have heard the chopper. It took me to an estate Dubh Craig where a Russian and his divers are salvaging a Spanish galleon."

"I did hear about that," Duncan asserted. "In fact, there was mention about it in one of the local rags; comparing it with that of the Tobermory so-called treasure. It was about the same vintage, and I did get a text that your Merlin was about to disturb this tranquil village last night."

"Anyway, I don't want to take up more of your time and I have queuing customers... We landed at a small private strip close to the estate house owned by a Russian called Eugene Banderoski. He is a marine expert, just like Michelle, and not a pleasant individual." David related seeing the helicopter's reflection and went on to say to Duncan, "I could possibly identify it if I saw a photograph."

"Well, I have no doubts, David, but if we need further verification, I'll dig up a pic for you."

"Well, to continue. Eugene offered to translate for the diver, who was conscious, and as we were taking him over to the chopper, he told the diver to keep his mouth shut, more or less."

"An interesting story, Dave," Derek cut in. "This could explain a lot."

"It certainly gives us something to work on," Duncan observed. "We have been holding out on you," he hesitated, "for we didn't want you to become involved. That's how we both feel. Jack was shot close by the Great Stack with automatic fire."

"I knew that there was some subterfuge, some deception, going back to the email and the stack of the five legs." The doctor looked pensive, "but I'm prepared to be patient and await the outcome. I may also live longer," he added. "I've already had a dress rehearsal with you, Duncan."

"That you have, David, but we were victims of circumstance."

"We'll enlighten you in due course, doc." Derek sounded sincere.

"Things are dropping into place," Duncan added. "We have to thank you for that astute bit of... what were your words? Ah, yes, 'subterfuge and deception'." He gave a chuckle.

David's parting word was, "Touché."

"I have a pile of e-mails, Duncan, and now confirmation that there could be a mystery chopper about." This was Derek. "I got several satellite pics of the Minch and the islands, which also show a chopper flying west in darkness, heading towards the Outer Hebrides. It wasn't showing lights. That, as you know, is not unusual in this part of the military training theatre, as there are often Chinooks with our Special Forces leaping out into 'dark air'."

"I'll have a look at those later, Derek."

"Fine. Now, deliveries. The camera should be here later today. I don't have to make any collections from Inverness now and the rib and other goodies will arrive at 4 am at the boatyard."

"That's service," Duncan congratulated him.

"Just as well we have pals in the mercenary DIY business, old man, otherwise I'd be bankrupt."

"I'm sure you will have spare trinkets for extra gratia bonuses."

"That's my hope, Duncan, but there's the more important thing of settling our personal dept..."

"I have similar sentiments," Duncan agreed in a subdued tone.

Michelle breezed into the room. "Hi, guys."

Derek's just been checking his shopping list. You may be able to play with your camera this evening."

"That's great. I have a gadget yen."

"You may get bored with seeing the eastern Atlantic day and night," Derek warned, "but it's vital that you report anything suspicious. It could be very important to Duncan and myself."

"By the by, as they used to say," she continued. "I had acknowledgement that David's cap arrived at the British Museum, also an E-mail from my contact. He calls it 'superb'."

"We're expecting the rib and other equipment very early, Michelle, at the boatyard. It will be a bore for you, but we will be back for breakfast."

"I guess I'll have plenty of time to see it later. If you give me a ring when you are finished, I'll put the coffee on."

"That's a deal," Derek agreed. "Also, those satellite pics I showed you. Some of the daylight shots are of the Outer Hebrides at the same latitude as that of the rib, the shot in the dark. Can you try and get some enlargements of a place called Dubh Craig, or its old name 'Varris'. You will be able to find it using the relevant Ordnance Survey map. We need these ASAP, close ups of the large house, with a farm building and a grass airstrip. There should also be a small harbour."

"Have you a map of the area, Duncan?"

"I possess all the maps of Scotland here." He turned round and from a shelf which spanned the width of the room, he handed her the folded map marked Lewis and Harris. "This is it."

She spread the map on the table and Duncan pointed out the area with a large forefinger. "There, that is the main house and I see that the barn is indicated by this small rectangle. This wee bay, just west of the house, is probably the natural harbour they use."

"Right, I'll get on to this," she said and added to Derek, "it's fantastic to get the high res. downloads."

"In case you are puzzled, Michelle, Dr David, who was on a medical call-out to the estate, by rescue chopper, stumbled across interesting information." He outlined the fresh developments.

"Well–well," she exclaimed, "what a break-through!"

Two large boxes arrived. Derek, who was now in the bedroom, came down and helped Duncan take them into the hall.

"I thought I heard a truck."

"I wish I could get deliveries as promptly; I've been waiting for a new strimmer for weeks. We'll take them into the office. No use advertising that we've entered the security business."

"No, indeed," Derek responded as he found a knife and proceeded to cut the banding off the cartons. On top of the contents in the first box was a large envelope marked 'Colonel Derek Hawthorne MC, BSc'."

"Is that the invoice, Derek?"

"I don't think so... He doesn't use invoices. I might have known," he continued. "It opens with a sub-title 'For The Mentally Impaired'. Bill Whiteman's sense of humour." Derek quickly scanned the document. "I have been told to put all the contents on the floor and there's a sketch with allocated positions. The battery?" he looked over at the other box. "It must be in there, Duncan, and also the remote pan head, recorder and lenses. Only when I do this, should I give them a ring to go through it with me? I'll have to get Michelle in on it."

"I'll leave you and put the quad on its trailer and rustle up a tool kit and we can take it to our boatyard in darkness, otherwise someone will spot it and think I'm poaching. Come to think of it, I'll look out some sleeping bags and a Gaz stove; we had better be prepared."

"You think of everything, Duncan, and before you disappear, I have been mulling over our strategy."

"Yes?"

"That news from David has shifted things up a gear. Even though I'm desperate to get back to the stack, I wonder if we shouldn't incapacitate the Russian contingent first. It could give us a window of opportunity..."

"A pre-stack strike?"

"Exactly. We are all geared up and could scuttle the black rib to keep the galleon company at bay and also give that chopper chronic indigestion."

"We'll have our work cut out," Duncan replied, "and we'll need familiarisation with your new boat... Radar?"

"She comes with everything, fully combatant, even a battery-powered inflatable and, like the rib, all possible camouflage both thermal and anti-radar treated."

"Sounds better than our service gear."

"Much. Oh, have you still got your face mask? The Russians make some sophisticated image intensifier equipment these days and we don't want your pale face on infra-red setting off alarm bells."

"I think it's under my bed along with an old German telescopic sight."

"Good. I'm glad that you still squirrel things away. Also in the box with the battery are three of the new generation NVGs. These night vision goggles are not much heavier than sun specs. I have also been told that this rib is designed for oil rig security – probably for people you know. But it's all high tech now. They even use magnets for scaling the rig legs."

"Tempus fugit, Derek. Soon we'll be obsolete."

"Not under the waves, I hope! Now to the present day, Duncan. Michelle can get the forecast and satellite weather charts."

It took Derek and Michelle two hours to master the camera and components and return them to their flight boxes. It would have taken them twice that time had they not had verbal instructions.

After a late dinner, where, surprisingly, no one said much, each being absorbed in personal thoughts, Michelle returned to the office to complete her chores.

Chapter 18

It was 10.30 pm before Duncan returned. He had had the quad fuelled and it occupied the spare space on the trailer which was not packed with rucksacks, ropes and black buoyancy bags.

Michelle came through from the office and joined the others in the lounge. She had changed into a one piece designer boiler suit in deep purple. As if on cue Duncan entered from the hall.

"My, you look the female lead for some romantic movie."

"Perhaps miscast," Derek interjected, but with a trace of admiration in his voice. "How about Chief Engineer on a Spanish galleon?"

"Oh, shut up, Hawthorne," she retorted good humouredly. "I'm not something you ordered from your shopping list."

"No, you're not, thank goodness."

Michelle appeared to be not too sure about the remark, but gave one of her smiles and addressed Duncan. "My primeval instincts tell me, Mr Laird, that we need fire. Shall

I light it, seeing as at least one of you observed that I'm appropriately dressed?"

"Great idea, my dear, and my primitive instincts tell me that I'm hungry again. How about some cold venison, red currant jelly and home made bread?"

"I can see you paying off Mrs Mathieson and exercising your hidden culinary talents."

"When the cat's away,.." Duncan chuckled. Mrs Mathieson was staying with her sister.

"Naughty, naughty." Michelle wagged a finger. "But I'll give you a hand," she volunteered, "and over supper I'll enlighten you both on weather, the estate of the enemy and rocks in the sea, which you can't see!"

"You both spoil me," Derek confessed. "But I have chores pending in cyber space."

"No worries, Derek."

When they had finished their repast some time later, Derek put down his serviette. "To risk repetition, MacGillivery, I must say, you have an idyllic life style. Living off the fat of the land, no wonder your getting soft."

Between them they demolished a large part of a haunch of venison. Derek neatly folded his host's monogrammed serviette and placed it on the table. "Don't you agree, Michelle?" He looked across at her on the opposite side of the table.

"I agree, a charmed life." She turned to Duncan who was sitting alongside with only the light of the table lamp reflecting off the polished purple heart table top, a darker colour than her boiler suit, and it gave his granite like features a cold, dark glow.

"I hope that the charm lasts over the next few days," he replied, taking a sip of Mrs Mathieson's elder flower wine. "Before you start your geographical and meteorological discourse, Michelle, I had better run through our plans and how you can fit into things. I've heard that the boat should be here a bit earlier than scheduled. We will unload it on to the ramp trolley, which as you know, runs on rails down from the floor of the boathouse. Lucky it is deep water in the Sound, so our trial in the dark won't be too hazardous. We will come back in alongside the launching slip. Afterwards, we will return for some sleep, if possible, and an early breakfast, 600 hours," Duncan said. "We won't get much sleep."

"What about our monitering camera," Michelle queried.

"We have to install it tomorrow and tomorrow night you will be able to view us heading west to North Harris in the dark."

"Then what?" she asked with a worried frown.

"Our plan is to immobilise the Russian's transport system so that they don't interrupt us. Also, you have to order a banner for the rib. Duncan will give you the size and where to get it post haste from Inverness."

"I'll sort it out later," she acknowledged.

"I could only spot one rib," Michelle interrupted, "but there were a couple of smaller boats, with outboards, up on the shore."

"Well, we shall see," Duncan said slowly. "Another one may have been in use elsewhere when the satellite went over."

"We have to put that chopper out of action and as soon as tide and weather are right, we will go to the stack and collect the artefacts, hopefully."

"It appears a good plan, but I hope no one gets hurt," she said. "Now, let me show you some of the Russian's estate." From her satchel she slid out prints spreading them on the table. Duncan assisted by removing the skeletal remains of what was once a prime hind haunch on to a nearby coffee table.

Michelle thought to herself it symbolic of the fragility of life.

"Well, this gives us more perspective," Derek announced. "Yes, I see a black rib on an outhaul. It seems about twenty metres from the end of that small jetty."

Duncan was looking with concentration at Michelle's work and observed, "It makes things easier for us as there's no accommodation at the bay for the diving crew, so they must stay at that log cabin by the estate house Michelle, can you pass over the magnifying glass on that side table. I want to search for any sign of security cameras."

"I've been thinking about that, Duncan. What has Banderoski to fear?" Derek asked. "Any nefarious interest, other than his own, would be concentrated on plundering that wreck. If he has electronic security and I'm pretty sure he has, it will be located on shore. I found out from the web that he got permission to salvage a wreck, a short way from the south west corner of Harris, where reefs, probably a continuation of Varris Point, arc underwater to the north west. I checked this from Crown Estates info."

"It makes sense, Derek. He could have a radar monitor, something like Michelle's camera, covering the wreck from his house and at the same time keeping an eye on his work-force."

"There speaks a true criminal mind," Derek observed. "It takes a genius to catch a genius, but I think you are right." He continued, sliding a print from the selection. "Is this the night satellite shot of their rib?"

"That is possible," Michelle confirmed.

Derek cut in. "Quite dramatic, those Russkis are able sailors."

"Indeed," Duncan agreed. "I wouldn't like to drive that rib in such a storm."

Derek now picked up the magnifying glass and was studying the bay just south east of the big house and barn.

"We'll have to check up on rocks, Duncan, but this bay," he stabbed the area with the pointed handle of Duncan's magnifier, "it looks a perfect place to anchor our rib during our raid, hidden from both house and barn, yet near enough to make a stealthy approach in the small inflatable."

Preparation continued and Michelle sat throughout, hardly saying a word, but she didn't miss a word either and had a glimmer of what drove these two. They were not unlike their predecessors, the Templars, with no room for sentimentality.

"My turn?" She turned to Derek. "The satellite weather prospects," she announced, picking out some stapled sheets, "look fair, but I'll get an update tomorrow evening. Wind south east which is a good sign. Oh," she added, "copies from the charts for your voyage into darkness are here. I mounted them in your laminator for protection, Duncan."

"How the hell I ever managed without you all these years I don't know," Derek said and put his arm round her waist.

They were satisfied that everything had been checked and decided to go to bed. Michelle headed for the kitchen first with the remains of their meal and to make up sandwiches and a couple of flasks.

"Duncan?"

"Yes," the big Scotsman looked expectantly, wondering what was coming next.

"There are two unaddressed items; getting into the barn and disabling the chopper."

"What do you suggest?"

"I saw the faint outline of what looks like a small window

on the south side facing the water, possibly a toilet. We could 'tape and break' to keep the peace, for it would be good to complete the op in silence."

"And the copter?" Duncan prompted.

"Inject sugar into the fuel, or a desiccated egg carton – an old Arab trick. Both gum up the works, or in this case the fuel pump filter."

"Possible, but I feel that we should also be prepared to inflict other damage, say the control box, which is in the back of the fuselage locker; buggering up the electronics could have a catastrophic effect. It would also be a good idea to give those two boats on the shore a sugary treat," Duncan added with a grin. "I must raid Mrs Mathieson's pantry."

The night was starry with a nip to the air. The Range Rover's headlights picked up the details of the track in a series of moving shadows, and the occasional field mouse scuttled across, playing Russian roulette with studded tyres. They approached the boatyard,

"If it's like this tomorrow night, Derek, "you won't require your GPS and auto pilot with all those stars to guide you."

"They worked for us in the desert, Duncan. Remember that stomp across the Sand Sea?"

"I thought it would never end," Duncan muttered, braking to avoid a red deer hind which shot across in front of them.

"Those were the days, my friend ...." Derek broke into song. Drawing up in front of the boatyard doors, Derek jumped out and opened up. Once inside, with the doors closed and locked, the strip lighting was switched on and the place sprang into life. The upper parts of the walls above the breeze blocks were of profiled aluminium; everything was a uniform white.

"What's the history of this place, Duncan?"

The reason that it's so remote is that the bay was an ideal location. Originally it was used for herring fishing. Later it was converted into the boatyard."

They had an hour to prepare for the arrival of the rib and unloaded the 4 x 4. They then tested the hoist for lifting the boat on to the ramp trolley cradle. Next, the other winch at the head of the ramp, on the level area, had to be checked. This was sunk into the concrete floor. It, too, was in good order. Its cable was attached to the boat trolley on rails and controlled the descent of the boat into the water.

"Looks as if it's all go," Duncan announced. "It certainly was providential that Torkil Mackenzie had both builders and mechanics check the premises regularly, but I suppose he's still hoping to lease it. In fact, I remember once that he was thinking of converting it into a sort of Outward Bound school."

"It would make a bloody good one," Derek agreed. "A kids' heaven."

Derek's mobile rang. "I'm just turning off on to the narrow road to your boatyard."

"Right, you'll see our lights shortly."

"I don't know, Duncan, if you overheard that brief exchange; the truck will be here in minutes."

"Well, we're ready. Let's open the doors."

Though it was a big vehicle, a low loader, it had a master driver behind the wheel. He switched on a bank of lights on top of the cab and swung the truck up towards the cottage and in one lock reversed the rear end into the boatyard entrance, then killed the lights abruptly. He jumped down from the cab and came over.

"Good morning, gents. I hope I haven't kept you waiting."

There were no introductions. He was tall, bigger than

Duncan, with a black woollen cap and what looked like a tailor-made one piece over-suit, probably with skiing ancestry. He looked Polish, but had no trace of an accent. Quickly, he appraised the set-up, the launching trolley, over-head gantry and the ramp winch.

"I'll reverse to below the gantry. The lifting strops are on the rib. When we hook up, we'll release the securing tapes and lift it clear. There are other packing cases which we'll unload afterwards."

He climbed back into the cab, took the truck forward a few metres, then reversed until the rib was directly under the gantry's lifting block.

"I wouldn't mess about with this bugger, Duncan."

"I'm glad he's on our side," was the reply.

The whole operation, including the packing cases, was completed in fifteen minutes. It was like a pit stop for leviathan trucks. The driver jumped down again to supervise things; that the beefy securing tapes retracted into slots under the deck of the trailer. He climbed back into the cab, put down the window and announced he would be back to collect the boat when they were finished. He didn't put on his head-lights, but drove straight down the track, using just two low fog lamps.

"It just shows you, Derek," said Duncan, amazed at the sudden silence, "what you can get done if you know the right people."

"I am witness to that."

Chapter 19

"You know, Duncan, I feel like a kid with too many Christmas toys. Which one will I play with next?"

"I'm the same, itching to see what goodies you have in those packing cases, even if it's not Christmas and if your selection is what I would have chosen."

"First, the rib's already fully fuelled up and ready to go, so let's get it into the drink."

"I've never seen one this big before, Derek, and the only place I've come across such an array of outboard power was in Columbia and Gib, with the drug cartels."

"They are expensive to run on full power. By the way, I hope that the fuel will be delivered."

"I told Innes, who owns the petroleum depot, that if he failed to deliver I'd personally come and break his neck."

"My," Derek said with approval. "Do I hear the MacGillivery of old now speaking?"

"Let's get suited up, Hawthorne, and grab some action."

"Hawthorne has to get a couple of the toys from that small case first." He returned in a few minutes.

"Put these on, Duncan, and I'll dowse the lights in the boathouse and lock up."

It took about forty minutes to get the rib into the water and free from its trolley. They were now afloat out under the stars. They could see almost as well as in daylight. The glasses were feather-light, unlike the military version they had used which could strain the neck muscles. Derek had read up on the rib's handbook from the internet and ran through things.

"It seems straight forward," Duncan observed.

"So far, old man, but there are a few mods. You can use any one or all of the engines. But engine three has a switch just above its control here on the console."

"And?"

"This is the button for 'Silent Mode' I mentioned. It means revs are cut to a tick over, yet there is still plenty torque. Let's try." He pressed the starter and immediately there was a slow murmur.

"I can hardly believe it," Duncan exclaimed. "It's quieter than the purring of my late cat!"

"And the engines are coated with the new anti-radar paint, just like our dry suits. Makes it a stealthy tool."

They went through all the controls, auto pilot, satellite navigation, followed by manoeuvres in the Sound, with all lights out. The sea was kind and the rib easily did 60 knots plus.

"Quite a machine, Derek. "A good choice, even at almost full throttle it's not that noisy. I meant to ask, but that big mattress thing lashed to the deck. Is that the submersible raft?"

"I guess so, the small inflatable is in that plastic cylinder we unloaded. We'll have a look at it when we get back and make sure the batteries are fully charged. We have 3,600 litres of fuel in the rib's tanks, but we had better top them up tomorrow, for it's a fair haul to Harris and back."

"Let's return, Derek, and put this thing to bed; an enlightening evening."

"Engage stealth mode for a couple of minutes, Duncan, and I'll give Michelle a ring. There's no point in her losing sleep as well."

"Good idea."

They tied up, then climbed one of four short ladders spaced along the length of the jetty for access up to the concrete, then crossed over to the containers. Duncan closed the sea doors and put on the lights. Shedding their suits, they systematically opened the boxes and removed the flight cases. These were all black and waterproof.

"Guess what's inside, Duncan."

"That one at the end should have LR printed on it: 'Last Resort', as well as skull and crossbones."

"Exactly my thoughts, man, when I was considering hypothetical hostile situations. I concluded that I would like a heat seeking missile in my rocket launcher when confronted with gun fire from a rib or a helicopter. As you know, back in 1986 the CIA equipped Afghan mujahhideen with these."

"I agree it's one of the most versatile weapons ever created. But I think it could be considered as overkill, though I know that you won't do anything rash."

They opened the case to have a look without saying a word. Duncan then closed it, snapping the heavy duty clips in place and moved to the next. To the uninitiated it looked innocent enough; about a dozen reels of what looked like washing line.

"We could have a rare Guy Fawkes night with this lot, Derek. Cortex always seems harmless and tactile until you attach a fuse."

"I have plastic, too, just in case we have a need for moving some rock inside the stack – heaven forbid!"

"In this lot, Duncan, are a couple of your favourite tools, an AK-47 and the .45 automatic pistol. An array of ammo is there and a couple of my own favourites, plus a selection of smokes, grenades, six CS gas rounds and a plasma cutter."

"We may as well take on NATO, 'old boy', as you call me." Duncan shook his head.

"I never forgot my Boy Scout days, Duncan. 'Be Prepared'. But then I thought it referred to contraceptives."

"Is this the inflatable?" Duncan pointed at a black container the size of a small beer barrel.

"Probably the most important bit of gear for tonight's show."

"I guess it could be," he agreed, turning it upright and releasing the four toggle clips securing the end. He slid the contents out on to the floor. There was a sudden swoosh as it exploded and inflated, causing them both to jump and laugh.

"Just as well that wasn't an IED (Improvised Explosive Device) or we would have been blown to bits." Derek gave another guffaw.

"I may have to change my underpants," Duncan confessed. "The instructions are on its floor in the transparent panel."

"I can't see the motor. Oh, yes, it's built into the rear, inside the inflation tubes. It's propelled by water jet."

"The batteries?"

"Let me see. Ah, there's a compartment in the bow tube: 'life three hours from fully charged'."

"That should do us."

"There's also a set of paddles, for slow operators – that's us."

"The battery gauge shows it's fully charged, so I think that we can trust them on that. After all, we do have the paddles."

"The other three boxes contain items for treasure recovery from inside a sea stack, Duncan, and are not of immediate relevancy. Oh, while I remember, there is something else. You remember the Tora Bora caves in the Afghan war, where Bin Ladin was supposed to be holding out? Well, special walky-talkies, operating on long wave, were developed which are much better than those used in mine or cave rescue. I managed to get my hands on three pairs of these just after we homed in on the Great Stack possibility. After all, we don't want to be sitting ducks inside. Anyhow, let's get some shut-eye, Duncan." He paused for a moment, looking serious. "I think it best to keep Michelle in the dark about our arsenal. It may give her ideas for diving for wrecks in the Aegean."

When they got back to Inverstack, they entered quietly. Other than Michelle there was no one else in the house. There was a note on the hall table in Michelle's handwriting, saying there were sandwiches and coffee in the lounge. This meal was dispatched with alacrity.

"I think you are right, Derek. I'll grab some shut-eye. See you in a few hours."

Derek went up to their bedroom and entered silently.

They arrived at the boathouse by 8 am. Duncan parked his 4 x 4 inside and Derek hitched the trailer to the quad and loaded the camera equipment.

"Are you two going to walk or take a lumpy ride in the trailer?"

"I think we'll hike, Duncan. What do you say, Michelle?"

"Yes, it's another good day."

"We'll lock up, Duncan."

As they walked along the elevated shoreline, the wonderful panorama of sea, mountain and sky opened up. Due west they could see the faint outline of the Outer Hebrides and a hanging sea mist wrapped round the higher tops. Once they moved out of the shelter of the bay, Sanday emerged from the green-blue sea. The water was calm and to the south above the shore, from where the noise of Duncan's quad emanated, a pair of golden eagles circled.

"I really love this part of Scotland, Derek. It reminds me of the Greek Islands, but colours are more subtle; that goes for the sea and the cliffs, too, with their thousands of birds. The light is always changing. It does not have the eye-watering intensity of limestone cliffs."

"You're right, but it's a strange comparison. I think it's something to do with the wildness of this place as well as another factor – mystery? That may come into it. Probably connected to the latitude and that lazy spring sun, as if it had all the time in the world to pass through the heavens, especially in winter, when it seems too tired to climb over the tops."

"My God," Michelle cried in delight. "You're waxing lyrical."

"It must be the air," he confessed, "or I'm getting soft."

Duncan had the camera ledge enlarged by the time they joined him. "Have a good walk?"

"What a superb day, Duncan. Have you left anything for us to do?" Michelle asked.

"You can see if the camera unit fits in its new hidey-hole and, Derek, where do you want the aerial?"

"I think that the place we selected before is best, but we can have a trial run." Michelle got the camera case from the trailer, scrambled down to Duncan and assembled it quickly. She then lifted the complete unit into Duncan's niche. "Looks good to me. Derek, what do you think?" she asked.

"Pretty neat. I'll get the battery and the other kit. Duncan,

can you manufacture a further ledge close to the camera for the battery. That hole," he pointed, "probably a rabbit burrow."

"No problem."

"As there's a spare battery, Duncan, we may as well commit both to the burrow extension and connect it in parallel, which will double the life and may save us a journey back here."

"I seem to recall," Michelle suggested, "that we can run a power check through the control unit at base. If they do happen to go down, we can always take one back for recharging."

Derek, who was now at the trailer, replied, "That's the best suggestion and two batteries will give us ample monitoring time. I'll connect this lot up and you get the base unit up and running, Michelle, then we can try for a signal."

"As you say."

The sun had mustered a new day's energy and it picked up highlights on the delicate wave crests. Duncan, who had his binoculars with him, checked the Sound for any spurious traffic every few minutes. He didn't want the surveyors surveyed.

"Right." It was Derek who called to Michelle. "Start running it when you're ready."

The first sign that things were operational was when the twin unit on the pan head swung round slowly and stopped when the lenses auto-focused on Derek's face.

"Oh, my goodness," she cried. "I can see a basking shark."

"I saw your ploy, vixen. What's the quality like?"

"Superb. The twin infra-red image intensifier system should deal with anything."

They gathered to view the LCD screen, which had an

anti glare hood. Using the joystick, she panned left in daylight mode to where the Great Stack was located and
zoomed in.

"That's something else," Derek exclaimed. "This HD is
a wow."

"That's progress," Michelle murmured.

"Can you find the geo entrance?" Duncan asked. In
seconds she pulled out slightly and panned right on to the
large red wall and followed it along and went in tight at the
geo's entrance. The tide was low so most of the opening
was visible.

"I think we can live with this," Derek announced. "Let's
fix and camouflage. I think we're on to a winner."

"One thing before we leave. Can you give me that big
cardboard envelope, my dear. Propped up at the rear of the
trailer."

She passed it to him with a puzzled frown. Duncan, too,
showed curiosity. Derek scrambled back down to where he
had been standing before and took a cardboard mount out
of the envelope.

"Michelle," he called. "Can you take a shot of this, full
frame for our friend?"

There was a loud guffaw from above. "Pure theatre,
Colonel Hawthorne. I'm sure that guillotine poster will make
Bill Whiteman's day."

Once the camera was set up, they returned to the boatyard, with Derek and Michelle hitching a ride in the trailer.

"The fuel has arrived," Duncan observed, shouting over
the engine's racket. He circled round in front of the doors
and the passengers jumped out. Derek opened up.

"It looks as if you will be running a tourist service to St
Kilda," Michelle observed, "with all that gas." Duncan
drove the quad to just inside the doors and switched off.

"To continue, Duncan," Michelle continued. "It reminds me of one of my colleagues. She was with her metal detector on farmland when she came across a rare pre-Pictish gold necklace. The farmer, who was a friend, had experience of finds on his property previously and had been inundated by hordes of stampeding treasure seekers. On this occasion he started a rumour that the police were digging for a body he was accused of burying."

"That's a cracker, Michelle. "Pity we can't use it, but the Manx Shearwater should do the trick. It's a cormorant that flies and feeds at night; a good excuse for our all night activities." He turned to Derek. "We may as well put the fuel on the trailer, Derek, it will save some carrying."

"Good idea."

Chapter 20

"Let's have a cup of your coffee. Michelle. I'll see what's to eat."

"I have a couple of flasks in your vehicle, Duncan. Shall we dine there? After all, you do have folding tables."

Derek, who had just closed and locked the doors, joined them. "Smoko?" he queried.

"Smoko, without smoke." Duncan stated. "I have biscuits, cheese, apples and cooked ham, again."

"Fair dinkum," Derek rejoined as he sat in the rear with Michelle.

After the snack. Duncan suggested. "It is better Michelle if you keep a weather eye via the camera from here, as you suggested. There's everything you need in the rucksacks in the far corner there, close to the switchboard. Stove, food. sleeping bags."

"It's already on the agenda." she replied. "I'll feel more involved."

"That's settled then," Derek agreed. "but let's do some chores before we return, put fuel containers aboard, top up the rig, secure the gear and put the raft on the jetty for the next excursion."

"What about our time table?"

"I'll answer that with a question. How fast can we go, Duncan? We don't know; weather's another factor. An hour, say, for our business on Harris? "We'll have a better idea when you, Michelle, get the Met tonight. I'd guess about a five hours' return trip, with luck, so we want to leave here as soon as it's dark. Are you happy with this. Michelle?" Derek asked.

"OK by me."

"If you check the camera signal from here, we will do our chores and sort out our kit.

"I'll wind up the quad and take it down to the rib," Duncan said.

The moving of the fuel took longer than expected. The necessary gear had to be to hand and secured and the small inflatable now occupied the last resting place of the raft. Duncan produced a couple of razor sharp ice climbing climbing tools. "They could be quieter than cortex for the demise of the black rib, Derek. We can tow it out over the deep trench close to the point of Varris and commit it to the deep. The twin motors will make good residual anchors."

"You certainly haven't lost your touch, you cunning old blighter."

"Let's pack it in, Derek. Mrs Mathieson will be back from Jemima, her sister, and has dinner scheduled. I left a note for her. Also, we had better see how your young lady is doing."

Michelle was in the back of the Range Rover with a camera base unit control beside her. "Hi, you two, have you got your cannons and nuclear devices primed?"

"It's people like us who keep peace in the world, Michelle. The 'Stop it before it starts brigade'."

"That's a good picture you have, girl. Anything of interest?" Duncan asked.

"Yes, let me show you. There are no less than three mega hard drives. If I want to check some past footage, for example, real time recording is not interrupted. Watch this, an immediate replay of any footage I may be interested in. This is a fishing boat, heading north up the Sound about ten minutes ago. Now I go back to the present and let me see…" She went wide, then panned to the right and there was the trawler which she immediately brought up so that it half filled the screen. They could even see a chap relieving himself at the stern.

"Is nothing sacred?" Duncan muttered. "We're going home for a meal. Michelle. Why don't we leave the camera here and you can put it back in the Range Rover when we get back? After all, we don't want to miss anything."

"Also, there is the shipping and weather forecast to copy." Derek added.

"It will he taken care of," she said, closing the case and, sliding out, took the unit over to where the remaining boxes were. Derek had the doors open and the lights off. Duncan moved the vehicle outside.

As they drove up the track. Michelle said "I'm using the remote aerial. Derek. I have it mounted in that slot vent in the corner of the boathouse."

"Good, we may as well leave it there meantime for the built-in antenna seems to work fine back at the house, should you want to use it there."

"Duncan, can you stop at that bush beside the track, just ahead on the left?"

"Anything you say, Colonel. Do you need a pee?"

Derek got out. He was holding a tiny green box with a spike on it. Going up to the bog myrtle, he inserted it in an opening between its stems and returned to the vehicle. "It's for you, Michelle, so that you won't be caught unawares.

Carry on, driver. It will alert you if anything comes up the track. We will hear it when we come back. Not only that, the sensor can differentiate between, say, a rabbit, a person or a vehicle and give a distinctive type of warning tone, which is time recorded by the monitor. It has a range of two miles."

"Handy little bugger that, Derek. Where did you get it?"

"Taiwan."

"That's good of you, Derek. I thought you had forgotten about it." Michelle said.

Mrs Mathieson had a guilt complex. When they arrived back at Inverstack, she told them that her sister had the flu and hoped that they had managed to look after themselves.

"Dinna fash yersel', Mrs Mathieson. We survived splendidly, but that doesn't imply that we are not looking forward to dinner."

"Salmon in white wine, Mr MacGillvery. It's a bonny fish you caught in the alder pool."

"Yum-yum," Michelle exclaimed.

After the meal Michelle gave them the weather reports. It looks like a 'go' situation, to revert to your jargon." She placed copies of the most recent forecast and a weather satellite pic which showed a high building to the west and light winds.

"Looks good," Derek commented. "We have time for a brief kip: what do you think?"

"I think," Duncan agreed. "that it's a damned good idea – a couple of hours?"

"Suits me," Michelle, giving a thumbs up, agreed. "I'd better take some warm clothes."

"There's a good selection of gear in the car."

"What more could a girl ask for."

"A benevolent millionaire?" Duncan suggested.

It was almost dusk when all three met in the lounge. Michelle now wore a dark anorak and brown over-trousers.

Duncan was in semi-Highland drag with a tweed jacket, corduroys and a fore-and-aft cap. Derek wore a navy blue pullover and jeans.

"We'd better get going," Derek suggested. "We can have a brew at the boatyard."

As they turned on to the single track, Michelle spoke. "I'm awaiting a bleep, Colonel. My life may depend on it."

He didn't reply, but a few minutes later the bug monitor gave a yelp like a stood-upon pup, accompanied by a panicky strobe light.

They wasted no time moving into the building and Derek locked up. Michelle switched on the lights and checked the camera recording. "Nothing to report," she called. "I'll set up in the back again, Duncan. Just leave it where it is. It gives a fine view of closed sea doors."

"Now we won't have any complaints, lassie. You'll have pictures of the sea to watch for the next few hours."

The two men went down to the jetty and put on their dry suits Michelle resurrected an old table from the small office and toilet which was built on to the side of the building. She also took out three folding chairs and from Duncan's gear extracted a camping stove, water and brew utensils.

In a few minutes Duncan and Derek came up to the coffee table dressed in uniform black, even their faces. They had various waterproof pouches attached to their waist-bands and the black neoprene hoods gave them a menacing look, not helped by a communication mike and face mask, with NVGs hanging loose from neckbands. Both had knife handles protruding from neoprene scabbards on their lower legs. Michelle felt a twinge of despair. She felt suddenly alien to these two that she loved in different ways. It was like seeing news footage of a riot squad about to engage with protesters. It gave her mixed and confusing emotions.

Long black fingers of shadows sneaked under the door on the jetty side of the building; the doors didn't go below the floor level. An enveloping darkness swamped them. But in moments, they could see that heaven had switched on its side lights; there was the brightening reflection of stars and they moved down to the rib.

"Can you cast off, Michelle."

"Sure, and good luck to you both."

They went down the few steps of the ladder into the boat and were immediately engaged in final tasks. Duncan then asked her to release the ropes and the engines throbbed into life. The rib eased out and Duncan gave a wave. Michelle burst into tears. She was annoyed with herself and her lack of control, and for the first time realised just how much she was dependent on Derek.

The two men made final adjustments to their gear, sliding up their face masks and pulling down their NVGs. They put their feet into the stirrups fixed to the deck and secured themselves with their harnesses to the console. Duncan was behind Derek astride the console, which could accommodate four people in line. The instruments were directly in front of Derek, dull green screens with Marine GPS navigation running and the co-ordinates already entered. A sophisticated radar scanned all before it like a circular detector on a dart board. They were in touch with personal radio coms that also carried feed back and scanning of marine and emergency channels.

"Are you ready for 'go', MacGillvery?"

"Wind her up, partner."

Chapter 21

The rib rose in response and gave the impression of low flying. No spine jarring thumping from wave to wave, but a smooth surge of power. It wasn't completely dark: there was an incandescence, a surreal quality. A sort of mysterious presence that Derek was trying to explain earlier.

"Keep your eyes peeled for flotsam, Derek. A few years ago this area was littered with thousands of Russian pit props which got swept off a freighter in a force 11. Mind you, it did solve a Hebridean fuel crisis at the time."

"My eyes are fixed on the radar screen. Duncan."

To their left the northerly point of Skye presented itself as a black presence. Duncan thought of Duntulm Castle, the ruins of which stand there on a promontory over the ocean, still haunted by the ghosts of the late chief, Donald Gorm, and his drunken guests. The castle changed hands on many occasions, for these were turbulent times. Way back, long before Donald made his mark, a Norse princess called Biornal was in charge, but later it was mainly occupied by the Clan MacLeod. It was all X certificate stuff, which makes modern nocturnal raids with mod gear seem a picnic.

They never saw a single boat on their journey. In fact, it would have been boring except for the relentless speed. Duncan spotted a small oil drum on the radar about a mile away on the port side, which gave them a new faith in mods.

Three hours after leaving the boatyard they had indication from the GPS Navigator that they were approaching their co-ordinates. In fact, they had noted landmarks on the starboard bow for several miles and ahead they could just pick out what was probably the beach showing slightly silvery with the NVG. Derek cut down to two engines and half revs. The rib now sounded almost silent and he knew they would have to switch to Stealth Mode shortly. A few minutes later they spotted a solitary light and a quick check with the map and GPS established that it was in facts Dubh Craig estate house. Derek immediately closed in to the shelter of the shore and the light disappeared behind outcrops. He switched to Stealth Mode and the boat seemed to be stationary, but it was still indicating six knots. The silence was spooky, enhanced by the call from the shore of a corncrake, a resident of the island, a bit early in the year for it he thought.

Within twenty minutes they were at their co-ordinates and the rocks, even with their glasses looked black – probably because they were. The echo sounder was showing ten metres below the transponder and Duncan vacated his perch and went forward to drop anchor. The engine was cut and there was only the sound of gently lapping water on outcrops some fifty metres away. As it wasn't yet high tide, Duncan adjusted the anchor line carefully. Derek swung the dinghy overboard, tied the painter to one of the rib's shackles and put the waterproof bags aboard, including their two black rucksacks. Despite their radio mikes, not a word was spoken. They got into the inflatable, which left little freeboard.

With powerful paddle strokes, they moved further out

leaving the beach on their right. At no time could they see that solitary light at the big house, but they could observe the top of the barn above the shoreline; it was beyond their side of the airstrip. Paddling absolutely silently, they got round the headland to where the Russian's rib was anchored and at the corner of the bay realised that there was less chance of being spotted on the rock than in the bay.

They pulled the inflatable on to a rock shelf. Duncan took out one of the large buoyancy bags and they shouldered their rucksacks. In minutes over slippery rocks, they reached the shingle shore and knelt beside the two beached glass fibre dories. They had thought, from Michelle's photographs, that they were clinker built. It only took minutes to adminster a sugary to the two engines.

They were now back at their own inflatable and put it in the water. Using the jet motor, they went out to the rib. It was big, not as large or as powerful as their own, but it obviously had a high cargo capability, if the buoyancy was anything to go by. It was moored on its outhaul anchor with a stainless steel strop and Duncan used the Supercut to sever it. He then handed Derek a nylon sling for a painter and at the same time tied the other end to a shackle on the rear tube D ring of their inflatable. There was a slight purring from the water as the motor started and, reluctantly, the nose of the rib swung round, then moved forward, away from the shore. It seemed ages before they reached their GPS location over the trench. They untied the painter and Duncan, who had one of his ice tools ready, moved into the rib. Starting at the bows, he systematically smashed the chrome moly blade of his ice climbing tool first into the four bow inflation tubes, making sure the entry hole was below water level. With powerful blows, he then sabotaged the two long baffled fuel tubes, followed by the four buoyancy chambers along the sides. He was now at the stem and it was becoming unstable. Derek got the other tool and together, one at the stem of the inflatable and the other at the bows, trashed the boat with ruthless efficiency. Once the initial pressure was lost, they could also puncture the top of the air compartments to accelerate emptying the chambers. In minutes, most of the rib was submerged and, with further sustained attack, it gurgled slowly into the murky depths like some deflated sea monster.

There was no hanging about and they were shortly rowing diagonally back to the shore line with the motor running to gain a suitable place to move overland to the barn, which was only about a hundred metres or so from the rocks. An indentation in the low cliffs proved an ideal depression for parking the boat. They put their rucksacks and two buoyancy bags on the rocks and scrambled ashore.

Luck was with them for though a waning moon had struggled over some of the higher hills of the mainland, a band of low cloud had providentially moved in from the south and provided a temporary screen. They made the most of this and reached the rear side of the barn. A quick examination determined that as well as the existence of a small window, obviously a toilet, for the elbow of a cast iron drainpipe was visible at ground level, there was also a door. This looked as if it hadn't been used for years.

Duncan pointed towards the window and they went back and placed their bags and rucksacks on the ground. The window was constructed with a single pane of frosted glass and a rather rotten-looking wooden frame, designed to open inwards. Derek took out a roll of black professional gaffer tape and, reaching up, criss-crossed the surface. Duncan had now a couple of wide blade angle jemmies with telescopic handles. He passed one to Derek and, using these in a ratchet motion where one, then the other blade, was inserted and outward pressure continuously applied, they got the Sharpblades into the recess of the sill and succeeded in crushing the bottom of it and interior sash latches. This allowed them to insert their gloved fingers into the gap and heave slowly, but unremittingly, outwards. The whole frame, glass intact, swung forward, but still held at the top. They stopped pulling, realising that the top of the frame wasn't going anywhere fast, but there was room to stand up beneath the angled window. They had managed to do this operation almost silently. A curtain of cobwebs impeded entry and they saw behind it a reinforced steel mesh blocking their way. This was attached to the inside wall. The heavy gauge was that used for reinforcing concrete. The cutters were put to work again and, with a series of dull, purposeful crunches, one after the other the six millimetre mesh segments were cut. Derek pulled the mesh panel free and put it on the ground, then moved in head first and in seconds had taken the gear from Duncan. He had a quick look at the barn as Duncan squeezed through the window.

The door which they had rejected for possible entry had large cut blocks of timber stacked against it. These looked like pier sections. Just as well they hadn't chosen that route, he thought. Duncan readjusted his NVGs which had got displaced on entry and studied the layout. The tail rotor of the helicopter was directly in front of them and the aircraft occupied about half the barn, which at one time had been used as a hangar for two light aircraft in the days when it was a commercial outfit.

Duncan noted that it was an Ecureuil/AS 550 Fennec, as he had thought. What a machine! And he felt a pang of remorse that he was going to be party to wrecking it. They had a prowl round. In the open area on the other side of the

Eurocopter was a compact Kuboto tractor with a tow bar attached, probably for moving the helicopter. There were items of diving equipment, including a modern ROV for underwater salvage and a pile of lift bags, hopefully for raising treasure. A stack of air bottles occupied the rear part of the barn or hangar and alongside was a large compressor and fuel tank. There were also machine tools, including a capstan lathe and a milling machine. Derek looked over several component shelves of spares, including some for the helicopter. He also noted with interest components for a BN-Britten-Norman Islander. Was this evidence of the plane that crashed?

They then examined the helicopter's fuel cap. It was made of aluminium alloy and was unlocked. Derek removed the internal gauze filter behind the cap, using a screwdriver. Then Duncan poured in a liberal helping of Mrs Mathieson's sugar, followed by Derek, who had shredded several cardboard egg cases and stuffed them in as well. Next, they moved to the helicopter's luggage compartment built into the fuselage. This was locked and Duncan had to pick the lock, which took several minutes. At the rear of the compartment, behind a light partition, they found the control unit which was the heart of the helicopter's electronic system. Taking out a plastic bottle of methylated spirits from one of the bags, Derek poured it over the relays and circuit boards. The cover was rapidly replaced, the door closed and locked up. Exiting by the window, they moved an old door against the opening as they crawled through, so that it covered the damage to the grill and window. Not that they felt it would make any difference, but at least it left the place tidy.

The voyage back to the boatyard was initially uneventful and they maintained a similar speed to the outward-bound trip. There was no sign of any other craft, but several transatlantic flights were high above in a myriad of stars, heading west and a waning moon spread a somewhat downcast light over the sea as if it was regretting that it would not be enjoying this balmy night much longer.

"Derek," Duncan's voice hissed over his earpiece, "five o'clock, 150 metres, a sub."

Derek had been almost hypnotically watching the radar screen.

"A bloody Trident, Derek."

Derek looked up and with his NVG could clearly see the nuclear submarine. "Good God, Duncan, I never saw a thing on the screen." In a reflex action he put the rib on to emergency power and it visibly shot forward and lifted further above the surface, putting up a big wake.

"You're wasting fuel, lad. That thing can easily out-run or sink us. I would revert to your normal suicidal pace if I were you. They'll know that they scared the shit out of us and are probably still laughing. They'll think we are Special Services and are not all that special. They have an unfair advantage of 40,000 rubber tiles covering it, which makes it almost impossible to detect."

It was still dark as they entered the boatyard bay. The engines seemed to relax as the revs subsided and Derek took it right up to the jetty. A voice above called.

"Hello, sailors, are you lost?"

Chapter 22

"We have to get back for breakfast, Michelle," Duncan said as they tied up the rib. "I'd better phone in to place our orders or Mrs Mathieson is going to be upset."

They drove to Inverstack, passing the vigilant bleeper, and Michelle told them of her activities. She was curious about the strange object off the port side of the rib as it was returning to the boatyard.

"Not as curious as we were, Michelle. It was the conning tower of a nuclear submarine."

"But how? Were you arrested? No, you couldn't have been. I saw you heading back, but there was an increase in your speed."

"There was," Duncan cut in with a laugh. "They didn't bother with us and probably thought we were one of a kind. Come to think of it, Derek, I wonder if there is an 'identification, friend or foe', an IFF on our rib?"

"Possibly, Duncan, considering that it was used for oil rig security. If so, that sub would have identified the rib right away and considered us 'friend'; just as well that we are honest seafarers!" Derek was removing his facial make-up and Duncan said "That, Colonel Hawthorne, is highly likely. Now, give me one of those swabs when you're through. I don't want Mrs Mathieson seeing me with this war paint. I had to use it sparingly. She'd wet her pants; coming back home singed was bad enough. After we get some sleep, we had better get back to the boatyard, re-fuel and check out the next stage."

"As you haven't said anything to the contrary," Michelle quizzed, "I presume that the mission was successful?"

"It was," Derek replied, "and did you see any other sign of life on the high seas?"

"Nothing, other than yourselves and that submarine."

"Here's your make-up swab, Duncan, don't run out of road. What puzzles me," Derek carried on, "why did the camera pick up the sub when I couldn't with radar? I guess it must be the automated image intensifier mode which it selects when it's more suited. It was a fine, starry night."

"That's the answer all right and those effective rubber tiles," Duncan replied. "I saw it OK with my NVG."

It was pre-normal breakfast time when they arrived back and Derek and Duncan took their kit into the office. Michelle had left the camera running at the boatyard in 'auto sensor pan mode'.

They had showered and changed when Mrs Mathieson wheeled in her trolley. She had little to say and was even a bit cool with Michelle. Obviously, she was miffed that she hadn't been told of Duncan's and his guests' movements and even more put out when no explanation was forthcoming. Her Calvanistic instincts told her that perhaps he was being misguided into nocturnal pursuits. In fact, she was accurate in her deductions. Heaven forbid she should ever find out that he had been party to breaking and entering, malicious damage to property, theft and several other misdemeanours under the Firearms Act too serious to contemplate.

"I think that I will have a couple of hours in bed," Duncan declared when he had finished breakfast. "If we go back to the boatyard for midday, we can make preparations."

"Good idea," Derek replied. He, too, had finished and nibbled a last piece of toast, more through pity than hunger. "How about you, Michelle?" he looked across.

"I'll go for that. It wasn't exactly strenuous watching that screen all night, certainly better than porn movies, but it was boring enough."

"You did well." he congratulated. "it's the stack next. We hopefully will have more trinkets than you will know what to do with. Also, our best tides are due about now; it's important we make use of them."

Duncan gave him a keen look which was rather incongruous minus his eyebrows. "I see you've been doing your homework, Hawthorne. The spring tides could make a great difference."

"I'll see to it." Michelle promised.

Two hours after Mrs Mathieson had cleared the table, all three headed back to the boatyard. Duncan had promised her that they would be back for dinner. Michelle, who decided to go with them, wanted to double check camera recordings and battery levels.

They passed the path bleeper. which now seemed a trusted friend. Derek went down into the rib to see how much fuel was required: the spare containers had not been used. Duncan, after replenishing some items from the boatyard store, felt a pang of remorse. He knew it would cause Mrs Mathieson anxiety that her domestic routine was upset, despite the reason given to her about manx shearwaters, which at the time seemed valid enough. but she probably saw through the subterfuge. He had overheard her speaking to herself when wheeling her way to the kitchen

"Birds that feed at night, indeed!" He could recall her spitting out the words with a degree of venom.

"Duncan," Derek called. "The rib will need six fuel containers. As you observed, it gets thirsty when its pulses start racing."

"I'll get the raft sorted out and make sure that I know how to work it, and the NVG batteries have also to be topped up, as does the inflatable." He added, "I'll hand down an extension lead, if you want."

"Right."

"I may as well use the spare containers on board, Derek. It's not that far to the stack."

"I guess so, but be on the safe side, he paused. "Yes leave two aboard for emergency?"

Derek unzipped the raft cover and, glanced at the instructions which were in four languages. By the time Duncan had re-fuelled and topped up the oil mixture tank, Michelle had come over from her monitors.

"The batteries are about 60 per cent, Derek, and there's nothing showing on the recordings as an alert. We had better change one in twenty-four hours or so. It was a quiet night for traffic, other than the sub scare."

"That was enough excitement for me."

"Before we go for our ritual brew," Duncan suggested. "How about running through the instructions for the raft that doesn't always float. I didn't take a proper look."

"Simple, really." his friend announced. "Basically, its a clever air mattress with low side walls and you can control it so that it sinks, yet stays level and will obediently remain at its programmed incognito depth if directed. It could, in fact, be used as a wide inflatable or as a submerged platform when linked up with look-alike brothers. It also could permit Special Boat Executive to walk on water, so to speak – which they think they can, anyway."

"Do I detect professional jealousy?" Michelle hinted.

"There was always a bit of inter-unit rivalry," Derek laughed. "especially between older members of the corps. Didn't you once tell me, Duncan, that some crannogs and island castles had submerged causeways for secret access?"

"Correct, but I don't think that they catered for drunken clansmen staggering home after the boozer closed, for they often took a zig-zag route under the water – I mean the causeways."

"There is a remote control for the raft," Derek continued. "You can call it up from the depths, just like those anti-submarine mines we used to sow in the Gulf"

"Things are getting too clever these days," Duncan observed. "l thought womankind was the greatest threat to man, but now I'm not so sure."

"What's that you are muttering about, MacGillivery?"

"Just a few idle thoughts, Michelle, about kind women who are a treat for men."

"Bastard!"

"Well," Derek announced. "I see we have run out of sensible questions. How about that brew and we can discuss tactics over biscuits and salami."

They were sitting round the small table beside the gas burner. Michelle had put out three mugs of freshly brewed tea. Duncan opened the discussion.

"What's more important, Derek, than a low tide, is fair weather. Hopefully, we can always squeeze beneath the arch and we also have diving gear, but we require a calm sea, for we don't want to be smashed against the side of the stack on our return from the geo in that rubber death tub, and we have to do it at night." He looked over to his friend, who was silent for a few moments. Michelle watched him, too.

"I see your reasoning. Duncan. It also hinges on opportunities. The weather forecast, the tide, and it would be good not to have the added complication of an under-water entry beneath the arch. However, let's start at the beginning. There are only three of us and we don't want to enlarge the party?" He looked at the other two. He saw by their demeanour that this wasn't an option.

"What do we do with the rib?" Duncan queried. "Michelle will be back at base to monitor the Sound. Eugene Banderoski is not going to sit on the beach and mope over his loss."

"Yes," Derek agreed, "but with ready cash he can buy a second-hand one on the island, so we have to get our fingers out. What I suggest is that we use Jack's dry dock to hide our rib, then go round to the arch in the inflatable, towing the raft. Our Operation Stack."

"Wasn't that what they used to call queues of trucks waiting at Channel ports?" Michelle asked.

"I trust we won't have to wait in line," Duncan returned.

"All we have to go on are Jack's pics, so we will have to expect problems." Derek warned. "Once inside, we will have to tether the raft at the bottom of the steps and lower the waterproof bags down."

"I wonder if we will be able to work with out head-lamps rather than NVGs once inside, Derek."

"That could be an option. We have both."

"Once inside, Michelle, you can contact us, using the long wave, two way radio. Again it is emergency use only, which means reporting anything flying other than birds and things that float or go beneath the surface and show an interest in the stack. If we have a pre-arranged code, say: 'St Kilda, force 8.' It will mean 'imminent prowlers'. Also, we should have a signal test once inside. Our message for this will be: 'St KiIda calling.' Your message should also be: 'St Kilda calling.'"

"Got that, Derek."

"Remember, this long wave can penetrate a thousand metres of rock and could be possibly picked up by submarines, and there's a listening station for nuke subs a short way south on Rona."

"Well, I think we are ready to go now, subject to weather. What do you think, Derek?"

"Yes, we must study the vital forecast. Are you happy with everything here, Michelle?"

"The camera batteries will be all right for another stint."

"And all the other batteries, too," Derek affirmed. "We may as well get back home and see if there are any developments."

"When they returned to Inverstack. Michelle went into the office to obtain a shipping forecast. Duncan was looking through a fistful of mail and a parcel lay at his feet. The housekeeper had pre-empted procedure and already had a fire burning. Derek had gone up to change. Mrs Mathieson, now apparently at peace with the world suggested a menu: king prawns, followed by saddle of local lamb and baked potatoes, with the usual veg. Dessert would be a special soufflé, the secret recipe of which she had learned when in the kitchen at Inverlochy Castle many years previously. The serving of this was a strict ritual with precision timing like piping in the haggis. But this was three hours hence.

Michelle slid into the room like a tropical breeze. Her perfume had an ambiance of extravagance. She was again wearing designer jeans, but these were a subtle green, not unlike the water round the stack. Above was a silk tunic with superb embroidery, which looked Caucasian. It had a matching headband with two interlocking hands which met on the crown of her head in a loop, which held her long hair as if it was flowing from a fountain.

"I think you guys have the luck of the gods. The forecast is still fine. 'Wind easterly, force 3, area of high pressure building from the west, no precipitation'. What more could a couple of geriatric pirates wish?"

"I could wish for one thing," Derek responded.

"You never think of anything else, you oaf. I'll get the detailed forecast later."

"Thanks, Michelle. At least I appreciate you," Duncan commiserated.

"Derek, about my test call to the stack." She turned to him; he was sitting now on her right. "What happens if there is no signal?"

"I'll try and call you with our pre-arranged message. If I don't succeed, I will try again shortly afterwards. Otherwise, we forget it and make contact on our regular radio, once clear of the rock prison."

"By the way," Duncan chimed in, picking up the parcel. "This arrived almost by return of post. It's…"

"'…a banner with a strange device', to quote from Longfellow's 'Excelsior'."

"Our Manx Shearwater poster." Michelle replied eagerly. "Let's see it." There was a hint of mockery in her voice.

Duncan freed it from its carton and rolled it out.

"It looks super." Derek exclaimed. "it's amazing how a good lie can cheer one up. I'll have to look up that damned bird in case we are questioned by a twitcher.

"Simple." Duncan explained. "It flies by night and looks

like an Exocet missile which got its name from the flying fish which often strands itself on boats."

As promised, Mrs Mathieson manufactured a memorable meal, culminating in her coupe de grace soufflé which was rushed in as if it was an urgent transplant. It tasted ethereal and slid down the throat as if desperate to please its creator. When she returned with coffee, Michelle complimented her.

"I think that was one of the best meals I've had in years." she enthused. "You should set up an Exotic Highland Restaurant, Mrs Mathieson. They would beat a trail through the heather to your door."

"That's kind of you, Miss Scott, but I like a tranquil life." And in the same sentence, turned to the laird with a trace of exasperation. "Will you be here for breakfast?"

"Oh, I expect so. It depends on luck, you know. One night the birds are feeding out towards the Minch, and the next they may be at Run or Canna. I'll give you a ring if we are held up."

Chapter 23

A low moon displayed only a segment of its beauty as a black veil covered the heavens. The stars didn't appear in their virulent brightness, yet there was no cloud. The big rib seemed to be ticking over, yet it shot across a polished black sea. Duncan felt he was aboard a chariot, a chariot of the gods, heading for a Valhalla of perhaps untold wealth, certainly an adventure, an Errant Knight.

There were side effects to his past life. His work meant that there were casualties. Where had his wanderings got him? he mused. There were, of course, effects to his life of adventure where the foe seemed always to have a stronger god. He was an unbeliever, or rather believed in himself, had his own self-contained code of conduct. There may have been a book of rules somewhere in his mind, which he abided by and found satisfactory, but it lacked the power of that 'being' behind everything, backing you to the hilt if you had the faith and you could conjure up support with a mat and a prayer, or even a war dance, then you got that jag of being the greatest. He was startled as Derek spoke over his earpiece.

"A rouble for your thoughts, old man?"

"Just thinking of the meaning of life and all that crap, Derek."

"I know what you mean. Probably the best remedy is to blot it out with more of the same – or a good wine. I have often regarded the pub as my 'local' anaesthetic."

"I think I'll go for wine and avoid becoming an alky. It could be tricky getting the rib through that channel, to Jack's parking bay," Duncan continued.

"I think that the channel is just wide enough, but we will have to watch the tide. We don't want to be sitting ducks in that hole. I would guess that we can have two to three hours inside the stack."

"I'm sure we will collect some momentos in that time."

With their NVGs they got a superb view of the cliffs straight ahead. They were making a bee-line for the geo. All of a sudden they were at the great cliffs. They reared up in a menacing way, now a great dark wall. As they nosed inside the entrance there was again that pale luminosity in the water of the channel and a ghostly ambience ahead descending from the open skylight. Derek pushed up his goggles to get a reality view, but all he saw was a uniform blackness.

Duncan was at the bow with a mooring pole, using it to fend off the walls of the channel. This worked well with only the silent mode engine ticking over; the other engines were raised. It wasn't so much the width of the rib that was problematic, but its overall length. However, they made it with only a few scrapes and tied on to Jack's black mooring ropes.

"I've put in a couple of camouflage nets, Duncan, to your left by the bow tube. We had better cover up for one of the security satellites is due over about now."

In fifteen minutes they had both the inflatable and the raft overboard with their gear and started to paddle out of the channel. Once outside, they decided to continue with this propulsion rather than use the jet engine; it was just as fast.

"I wonder if Michelle has us on her screen. I'll give a wave with the paddle."

"You know, Derek, I had a brainwave. We could use semaphore to communicate. I once took a course on it when I first joined the Marines, but I guess I'd be a bit rusty now."

"And I thought that I had the franchise on bright ideas."

As they came round the stack they felt the rise and fall from the tide coming through the channel, as if it were saying: 'It's not always like this, consider yourselves privileged.'

There appeared to be only about fifty or so centimetres between the water and the arch, not enough for even a small dinghy, but their inflatable could possibly squeeze beneath and they would have to lie on their backs on its floor and propel themselves in by pushing on the rock ceiling with their feet like that boatman did all those years ago, and they also had the advantage of the jet motor. Though they both had their diving gear, the upside down option appealed to them. The squeeze through was exhilarating. Neither had ever experienced anything quite like it.

"It's between a water bed and a hard place," Derek exclaimed as they exited into a huge chamber.

"A bit like cave diving between sumps, wondering if you are ever going to get through. Didn't you do some of that in those French caves in the Calanques?"

"I did, but I was a novice with a master speleologist. I was, so to speak, out of my depth."

"Bloody hell," Duncan exclaimed. "I scraped my NVG on that rock ceiling, but the lenses seem OK."

"They are not so good in here. We'll have to get a candle lit. Ah, we are at the steps." He switched on his headlamp and everything burst in to life as the NVG kicked back in.

"Hey, what a place, Derek! 'The Hall of the Mountain King.' Very Wagnerian," Duncan added, getting out of the inflatable on to a slippery step.

"In fact, it was Grieg who wrote the piano concerto for Ibsen's *Peer Gynt*."

"I stand corrected, Colonel, but it looks Wagnerian to me."

"I have to agree."

"St Kilda calling."

The call was so sudden, but at the same time expected. It seemed completely out of place. Duncan took the miniature long wave radio from its waterproof pouch on his waistband.

"St Kilda calling."

"It seems to work well," Duncan observed. "Let's get the ball rolling, Derek. We've got a tide to catch."

They found a rock bollard to tether the two crafts and started to pile their equipment on a higher step. Then they went to explore the upper part, carrying most of their gear with them. Faithful to Jack's photographs, the pictures were converted to reality with the steps getting progressively smaller and, after dropping their gear on the open area behind the wall, they opened the massive door.

"Hold on a tick, Duncan. I'll get the candle lights on up here as well. They'll give enough light for the NVGs to operate properly, but we may be better just using our headlamps in here as we suspected."

"I agree, and it gives us more peripheral vision."

This was the case. The walls reflected an amazing amount of light. Also, the chamber was bigger than they had expected. At the back they could see a passageway. But they lit the candle lights and had also a couple of high-powered hand searchlights. Now it looked like a stage set.

Everything was for real. Random piles of artefacts, familiar to them from studying the photographs, mingled in the dust of their original bags or containers: crucifixes, necklaces, vases and other items so far obscured. There was no time to conduct a proper inspection and they rapidly stowed them one by one carefully into the black bags and closed the waterproof zips. They then took them to the top of the steps in a daze. Some of the items looked priceless, especially two superb ceremonial swords, with silver engraved scabbards and diamond encrusted hilts.

"Let's have a quick look round before we load this lot, Duncan. Remember, Jack lost his battery power and we don't want to miss anything."

They moved through the main chamber and entered to the back of the excavation. They knew it was a man-made cavity, more like a tunnel, really, and they could see tool marks on the rock. This led back for some ten metres into another cave about the same size as the first. Here, several ancient rickety shelves still stood along one wall; some had collapsed, the others looked well past their use by date, their contents untidily scattered on the floor amidst debris, looking as if wood worms had had a field day. There was also gold coin glinting seductively, after waiting all these years, and numerous beakers similar to the design of Dr David's ornamental cap.

"Good God, Derek. This is unbelievable!"

"This deserves another visit. I think we should hot foot it."

"I agree. I'll go to the bottom of the steps and you lower a bag at a time."

Duncan went down with a rope end and tied it off to the raft. Meantime, Derek clipped the first bag on. It took ten minutes to load the raft, then the netting cargo cover was fitted. One remaining bag had to be stowed into the inflatable.

The various candles and torches were put in the one remaining bag and Derek returned to the inner chamber to take some pics. When he got down the steps, Duncan was already in the inflatable and the raft set to float, giving an overall clearance of fifty centimetres. Derek scrambled aboard, the jet engine was started and the slack taken up on the painter.

Progress was slow due to the weight of the cargo; they had to assist with paddle power. Though the water seemed lower during the stack visit, the raft was adjusted further to allow it to clear the arch. It seemed an eternity getting out beneath and they had again to deploy feet power to gain the stack channel. Here they extinguished their torches and returned to NVGs. Then they raised the raft with its remote control and headed round under the stack's east face en route for the geo.

Considering the weight of the cargo, their progress wasn't too bad, though they felt that the raft was unstable with a centre of gravity which was beyond its limitations. They didn't want to tow it deeper in the water due to drag for, had it been rougher, it could have turned over and that meant that it would be slower to tow.

"I think, Duncan, that it would be sensible if we moored the raft at the entrance to the geo, as that would make it easier to transfer the cargo and also give us more freeboard for taking the rib through the channel."

"Makes sense. I seem to recall a boulder at the start of the channel where we could leave it."

They were engrossed in tethering the raft and had no sooner done this and adjusted the buoyancy to 'Surface Level' than they heard the heavy twin engine of a helicopter. This was simultaneously accompanied by a warning from Michelle on their working frequency: "St Kilda, force 8."

Duncan recognised it as a Merlin and from inside the geo.

"It's OK, Derek. It's an SAR chopper from Lossiemouth.

Must be a maritime call-out. Probably John Simpson driving. I think he's on night shift."

The two men moved up the channel in the inflatable, using its small motor and stopped at the rib. Once aboard, they released the ropes and decided to push the rib out of the channel, using the paddles as there was a risk of fouling it if the stealth engine was lowered. There was a marked difference in the tide level. They were glad that they had done this for it actually scraped the sides of the channel at one point. They realised that it was a close thing and both mentally put this fact in their memory banks. After the cramped set up on the inflatable, getting everything aboard the rib was wonderful. The bags were neatly stowed midships and secured with the raft upside down over them and the inflatable angled behind. Both were lashed to cleats. The boat stole out cautiously like a rabbit from its bolt hole, a stealthy shadow on a moving ocean. Then they saw that the stars had been turned up to maximum. The three other engines swung down on their pivots and broke into song. It was as if a great artist had raised his brush and petulantly drawn a white swathe east north east, creating a white line across an otherwise blank canvas.

After the slow progress towing the raft to the geo, the journey in the rib was exhilarating and seemed only to take minutes before the long, sinister craft whispered alongside the jetty. Michelle was standing at the second ladder. She had both hands cupped over her eyes trying to spot the rib, yet it was only about fifteen metres away and she could feel the pulse of its engines. Then there was silence; she couldn't hear the stealth engine. A voice called out.

"Can we have a rope, Miss Scott?"

The tail end of a climbing rope snaked down and she called "Have you got anything to declare?"

"You will be pleasantly surprised, my girl," Derek responded, cutting the engine, Duncan tied off on to the bow cleat.

"I'll go up top, Derek, and hoist the bags. We'll need to use the trailer as well as the rear of the 4 x 4 to get everything back to Inverstack."

"Hi, Michelle," Duncan greeted her as he joined her. "Great to see you again."

"I wish I could see the same," she replied. "But I don't have magic glasses."

"They must be back in the office. Use your headlamp meantime, but wait until I lower the sea door."

"I'm sorry, but I opened it in the forlorn hope that I could see you coming in."

"That's OK. Meantime throw a stern rope to Derek. He'll tell you where he is."

The silence of the boatyard was broken by the massive door descending. To Michelle, it seemed to signal the end of an act. The Range Rover started up and Duncan hitched on the trailer, then circled round to stop above the rib. There was still a couple of hours of darkness in hand as they loaded the bags and tidied the boat.

Instead of taking the drive up to Inverstack House, Duncan cut off on a small road, an off-shoot from the drive, which took them to the back of the house. Here was the old stable block, part of which had been converted into two large double interconnecting garages.

"This will be our treasure store," Duncan announced, getting out. "I imagine you will have many happy, hours here, Michelle."

"I just can't wait," she breathed. "It's incredibly exciting."

Chapter 24

Squadron Leader John Simpson had always been interested in problems. Based at Lossiemouth, he was a very experienced pilot. Search and Rescue had been a good move for him, for he had seen action in various theatres and preferred the forces of nature attacking his aircraft to gun fire and missiles. When Duncan MacGillivery asked him about helicopters flying in the Minch area, he was curious. That Eurocopter he spotted was out of place and there was no official record or flight plan. It was also a special aircraft with superb high altitude capability, an attribute that wouldn't be of much use over the eastern Atlantic, he thought. Then there was also that bends evacuation to Dunstaffnage Hypobaric Unit with a Russian diver and the salvage work on a wreck close to Dubh Craig estate.

He was returning to base after a call-out was aborted to the west of the Outer Hebrides. He decided to change course slightly so that he would fly over the estate buildings from the north west at about one hundred metres altitude, which meant that the Merlin would be hidden on the approach by a hillock just short of the estate house. He switched the two forward cameras on as he passed over the top of this high ground and, suddenly, the old estate house appeared below with a modern log design building close by. He spoke to the co-pilot.

"Just checking. This was where we picked up the diver with the bends. There, ahead, is the strip which was used for island flights years ago, it was also a basking shark hunting station."

The doors of the large barn were open and two heavily built men were closing them, quite quickly, he thought, but they didn't look up. John Simpson and his co-pilot saw a helicopter in its garage.

"That's a chopper in there, John," Malcolm, the co-pilot remarked. "Salvage must be a lucrative business."

"Yes, it looks like a Eurocopter, possibly one which we saw some time ago close to Sanday." He never added that he had run a check on it.

Down in the Vestate house, comment wasn't so restrained. Eugene Banderoski had dashed out to the glass fronted porch of the house and watched the big machine as it flew south eastwards over the barn. For a moment he had a feeling of despair. As he didn't have a view of the barn doors from the house he took his walkie-talkie from his waistband and ran down to the barn. He barked in Russian.

"Igor, were the main doors closed?"

The reply was immediate. "Yes, I think that we got them closed in time."

"I certainly hope so."

When he reached the barn he got a first hand account of what had happened, but it was obvious to him that the Merlin crew had had, a view inside the open door. He realised that this was no jolly, but a premeditated action to gather information.

"Has Milosh got any further with running repairs, Igor?" He addressed his powerful group leader whom he had known for years.

"Yes, he's over at the lathe."

"In the future, Igor, don't open the hangar doors unless the machine is about to fly and then only at night." He paused in mid-stride. "Also, get rid of all evidence of the Islander spares, manuals, etc. It was used for drug running before I got it, so it can't be easily traced. It was too bad that Andreas crashed it in that storm. He was a good pilot.

"At least we managed to recover the Templar treasure, or some of it," Igor remarked.

"Yes, we should all be very wealthy when that comes on the 'silent market' back in Moscow."

"I'll see to the disposal of the evidence."

"Another thing. That second hand rib you looked at in Stornoway. Are you sure it's in good order?"

"Yes, excellent, about six months old. The owner had cash flow problems and you got a bargain. He found too late that tourists are not keen on the roller coaster ride to St Kilda. The single 250 HP Yamaha is barely run in. It will be delivered tomorrow."

"Good." He strode into the barn. "Morning, Milosh. Have you an update?" Eugene looked at his top mechanic. A small man with a big head would be a good way of describing him. Certainly, his head was larger and some-how balder than normal, but it housed a brilliant brain.

Eugene had lost all hope of beating him at chess and though Milosh could possibly have attained a foothold to be a Russian great, though he was a Czech by birth, he regarded the game as purely recreational. At one stage in his career he had been chief mechanic for an international car manufacturer with a participation in Formula 1 racing, but he fell from grace when he sold trade secrets to a rival company to fund his habit. In his varied career he spent time as a helicopter engine designer with one of the leading French aero space firms. A talented, if misguided, man.

There was nothing charitable in the fact that Eugene had taken him under his wing on condition that he said 'do svidaniya' to coke and spent an extended period in one of the most remote corners of Britain and just about as far as he could get from a supply source. Also, there was a warrant for his arrest in Greece for illegal trafficking in stolen aircraft. His criminal history, however, faded into insignificance when compared with other members of Eugene's crew.

"I am having replacement electronics for the aircraft which was sabotaged with metholated spirits; they are being sent from Vienna," he informed Eugene. "What's interesting is the fact that they could have wrecked the Fennec in seconds, had they wished, for they are obviously professionals."

"Yes, that's odd. It's almost a terrorist strike, simple, silent and effective and one would think a delaying tactic… to gain time, I wonder?"

"As I told you, Eugene, it was lucky that I was the first person into the hangar after the raid and suspected something was wrong. I saw the old door covering the rear window and knew it was sabotage. I thought of the fuel and looked at the fuel cap. At first, everything seemed in order, as I told you, but then I saw that the internal filter had been trashed and found several grains of sugar on the concrete. It was obvious what had been done." He continued, now sitting on a high stool beside the capstan lathe and idly picked up a parallel reamer and started to fiddle with it. "Today I managed to drain off the main fuel tank and in so doing also discovered traces of a cheap cardboard in the residue. I don't know if you have seen this before, the mulch, egg cartons, are favourite." He cleared his throat. "To me that suggests – persons familiar with Africa and the Middle East, where it's popular. Possibly with terrorist connections or," he paused, "those who fight terrorists. A Special Service Unit?"

"You could be right. I prefer your last hypothesis."

Milosh looked over at his boss. It was almost a concerned glance.

"You can't fly the aircraft as it is, Eugene, and we don't have the facilities for dismantling. Furthermore, you can't switch to the auxiliary tank for forty-five minutes extra flight, even if I could devise a means of topping it up as that supply feeds back into the main tank. I'm going to blast compressed air through all the fuel lines and wash out the main tank with kero and that may do the trick, but it will take some hours to reconnect the replacement central electronics unit. Don't hold your breath, but I may get it back to the skies quicker than saboteurs think, but it won't have an MOT."

"You have been busy, Milosh. Had any sleep?"

"Not yet."

Eugene's office was in the estate house, though a smaller office, used by Igor, was attached to the log cabin building. Igor had returned to catch up with work. Eugene entered to discuss tactics.

"Igor, we have to sort out a work schedule," he addressed his chief diver who was about to finalise the delivery of the replacement rib.

"Yes, things are in a bloody mess," Igor agreed. "We need this new rib urgently as we have to get a compressor to the galleon, the helicopter has to be repaired and what about Stack Sanday?" He didn't call it the Great Stack.

"I have a bad feeling about that," Eugene mused in his

thick accent, looking from the window of the office across the landing strip to the open sea. "I think we made a mistake killing that diver and where did he come from? There was no sign of a boat. He must have been dropped off there, but that doesn't make sense either."

"It's possible that he was working alone, perhaps with no interest in Stack Sanday, or he may have left his boat in a cave or some hidden bay, but I can't think of any. Why don't you check it out on the charts and sailing manuals?"

"Good idea, but we may have to return to Sanday before we re-commence work on the wreck." Eugene went over to the main house, deep in thought. Isabella Abalakova, his girlfriend, looked up as he entered the lounge which she had furnished in a Bohemian style. She was an ex-dancer of the Bolshoi Ballet, lithe dark and quite stunning.

"An uninvited visitor, Eugene?" Her pencil thin eyebrows arched as she smiled.

"RAF nosey parkers," he spat out. "I think our cover is blown. That bloody sick diver was one of the problems. It may be dangerous for you to stay on here. There are too many strange things going on, especially at night!" He moved across the room to the door leading to his office.

Isabella went up the stairs to her bedroom deep in thought. Her boudoir, for the room deserved such a title, was sumptuously furnished with some superb antique rugs on the walls and a surfeit of embroidered cushions on every flat surface, but especially gracing the large four poster bed, it was as if violence or violation was imminent. She was taken aback at Eugene's outburst for she had never seen him so agitated. Normally he was cold and calculating showing less emotion than the jelly fish that littered the beach. She glanced down at her toe nails, then examined them minutely, but she wasn't really observing them, more considering her options. Return to Gorky? At least, she thought, she wouldn't be under house arrest there for she hadn't been allowed beyond the limits of the estate since she first arrived several months previously. The fact was that this security was part of Eugene's plan for the salvage operation. She reassured herself that these restrictions applied to the divers as well. She had to give him the benefit of the doubt, for she was aware that the forces of greed know no bounds, especially in the salvage business. There were also the incidents of the missing rib and the sabotage of the helicopter. Yes, it may be time to go, she concluded, and not just for her health.

Chapter 25

A feeling of excitement prevailed over the breakfast table. It was as if an important event had occurred and things wouldn't be the same again. Michelle had only time for a quick look in a black bag and shook the dust and debris from one of the objects, a diamond studded bowl, the like of which she had never seen described before in any archaeological tome.

"Gosh, I was famished," she said, putting down her knife and fork, "and weak at the knees," she added. "If the rest of the collection is anything like that first item, you've struck a bonanza. I'm almost frightened, knowing what some people would do to get their hands on the find."

"You're right there, Michelle," Derek replied.

Duncan deliberated. "We can register the find legally. Treasure Trove, you call it. Now, I'm not the legal owner of the Great Stack, my friend, Torkil MacKenzie-Baron is, as well as Sanday. It's part of his estate bequeathed by none other than King Robert the Bruce. But before I risk boring you further, I feel that what I have to say is pertinent, but legally a possible minefield. At one time way back the island was probably owned by the resident islanders or another clan overlord. Anyhow, they did have their own parliament, at its head a queen who was the oldest widow on the island. They met daily to discuss local problems. As recently as 1848 twelve families lived there until the great potato famine of 1848 forced the population to emigrate to America."

"You know, Duncan," Michelle laughed, "I told you, you could make a hit lecturing on popular Scottish history."

"That may be, lassie, but I think it's more lucrative locating Templar goodies. Anyhow, before I was interrupted, I was going to say that the location of the stack is interesting. It is essentially a mini island, for it's surrounded by water and the Crown Estates, owned by the Queen, defined in Scotland 'the land between mean high water of spring tides and mean low water of spring tides' as theirs. The stack is surrounded by water, as you know, we found the hoard above 'mean high water spring tides', and as I just stated it is part of Torkill's land."

"Interesting, Duncan," Derek responded. "Michelle says that all finds must be registered with the Treasure Trove Unit at National Museums of Scotland."

Michelle cut in, "Yes, that's the case now. This find is so important it will come under the umbrella of the National Museum in Edinburgh."

"Our adversary at Dubh Craig in Harris will probably make more laundering his find abroad, but that's illegal," Derek added

"Anyhow, there's a hell of a lot to do," Duncan chimed in. "You probably have the biggest task, Michelle, photographing and compiling an inventory. Derek and I can return to the boatyard and get batteries charged and the rib refuelled."

"That makes sense. I'll check on the weather again. Oh, by the way, there's some good footage of the SAR helicopter flying past the stack and of someone making rude gestures with a paddle. It looks as if they were heading up that well known creek!"

"Can you order a big roll of bubble wrap, Michelle?" Duncan asked with a chuckle. "We'll need masses for wrapping our presents."

"Will do, big man, it's already on my list as well as some strong boxes or containers."

Duncan spoke. "Before we do anything, Derek, we had better get our loot out of the black bags; we'll need them for the next consignment. Oh, another point, the garages come under Inverstack security. There are cameras in both places and the steel doors are fitted with deadlock bars. The only access, other than the main doors, is via another steel internal door to the house which goes through an old potting shed connecting both."

"You think of everything, MacGilivery," Derek complimented him.

"You must thank my great uncle that I never knew. He collected works of art and it was his store."

"I'll be able to go to work in my slippers," Michelle observed primly.

Before they started their task, they made a resolution not to start examining items in detail or, as Derek remarked, "Otherwise we'll be in the garage for days!"

The extent of the recovered treasure was beyond their dreams, and after they had everything neatly laid out in some order, Michelle was the first to speak.

"Now that we have completed this part of the job, I would like to say that this could be one of the largest treasure trove discoveries for years. I am sure of that and there is still more to come from what you say. But I'm tempted to pull out now. Is it worth all the extra risk?"

Derek and Duncan looked at each other. There was a pause.

"If we call it off, I, personally, would regret it for the rest of my life and I would be haunted by the images of those two swords we left behind. Not just for their value, but the fact that we could have prevented some wealthy Russian collector acquiring them."

Duncan seemed hesitant to speak initially. In fact, Michelle and Derek looked at him expectantly.

"I do think we will be taking a greater risk on the next visit. Eugene Banderoski is no fool. He will expect us to go right back to the stack and will have calculated how much we took on our first visit, taking into account the limitations of moving it, cargo space, time, weather, which are all major obstacles. I also think that you're correct, Derek; we should try and retrieve the remainder of the hoard for posterity, for once it goes out of the country, it won't be seen again except by some oligarch to ogle privately, as he knocks back his vodka."

"Let's go to the boatyard," Derek voted. "We're wasting time. Will you be OK here, Michelle?"

"My beloved," she grinned. "I could spend the rest of my life going through this lot!"

The two men went about their tasks with silent precision. The replacement battery was taken out to the camera position and all other batteries put on charge. As well as topping up the fuel tanks, the raft was given the once over and the built in compressed air cylinder re-charged. Meticulously, they checked their arsenal, ensuring everything was in its place, oiled and working perfectly. They did this with a systematic thoroughness of long years of practice; nothing was left to chance. Lastly they ran over the camera footage in fast visual mode and only switched to normal play when the paddle scene and the helicopter appeared. They were impressed with it. Putting it on 'guard mode' again, they locked up and drove back to Inverstack. The roads were quiet as the tourist season had not yet started. They noted in the blue sky the tell tale sign of cirrus stratus. After they had parked at the side of the house, they immediately went through to the garages and knocked on the door. Derek called, Michelle."

"That was quick. It seems you have only been away a couple of hours."

Derek lowered his head slightly and touched his forehead in a good rendition of Commander John Lightfoot.

"He that toils with diligence
Has no idle thoughts."

"Oh, not another," Duncan groaned. "I see why you are a fan of corny Aesop. In fact, I looked him up for you." Duncan gave one of his deep guffaws. The end part of one of his saws runs thus and is reminiscent of that piece of firewood you found: '...one day in the greatest rage he went to the Wooden God and with one blow swept it down from its pedestal. The idol broke in two, and what did he see? An immense number of coins flying all over the place.'

"Good God," Michelle moaned. "It's infectious, one is as bad as the other!"

"We had to come back to dine, Michelle. I trust you are going to shower and dress for dinner?"

"I'm going to get disinfected, before I fall foul of a lurgy from the middle ages – and I don't mean the over forties!"

"Have you found anything outstanding worth reporting?" Duncan looked along the now neater and cleaner rows of crockery and ornaments?

"Have I found anything we should discard would be a more pertinent question and the answer is no. The knights selected everything for its value and quality. You can realise how they were such successful bankers."

Mrs Mathieson had been contemplating the interest in the garages all of a sudden. At least it caused her less consternation. Anything was better than chasing Manx Shearwaters. She hoped that the latter hadn't come to the attention of the locals. It was convenient that the bird flew only at night.

Duncan and Derek were sitting by the fire when Michelle came in.

"You certainly look scrubbed clean," Derek said approvingly.

Duncan retorted, "You've no finesse, Hawthorne. That suggests carbolic and bleach to me. I detect a wafting fragrance, like wild flowers in the machair."

"What a nice thing to say, Duncan. I don't know why I associate with this oaf." But she gave one of her smiles to her boyfriend. "Anyhow, down to business," she said, sitting down in one of the big armchairs. "The forecast is still OK for the moment. Force 3, veering westerly, which probably will feel like a full gale in that small inflatable, but I suppose that it can't sink – unless it's riddled with bullets."

"Tut, tut, girl. Think positive. We were brought up with bullets, not sweets."

"Let me have a look at the chart," Derek requested. "I thought so, that cirrostratus nebulosus told us this in the afternoon. There's a depression building to the west."

Duncan butted in took it from him. "It may still give us a window. If we don't take it things could change."

"We could always come back if need be."

"Right, that's settled. Are you prepared for an all night vigil, Michelle?"

"Yes, I'm looking forward to it provided it doesn't get too exciting."

"Midnight start?" Derek looked at his two companions. They nodded.

It felt almost routine now, leaving the jetty in total darkness. What stars there were, were lacking clarity and the NVGs were short in sharpness. There wasn't much of a swell, more as if a powerful force was getting restless. Derek thought as the rib zipped across the surface that they may have to work for their rewards this night.

The tide was not ideal, but starting earlier would help access into the geo channel – and out. They left the raft on a short length of rope tied to the anchor rock to collect when they came back through the channel in the inflatable. Both were determined not to leave their return too late.

It made a tremendous difference knowing exactly what to do, where to fend off the boat from a submerged rock and other little observations from the previous trip. They had run through their checks on everything they would need and upon reaching the inner pool, tethered the rib with Jack's ropes. Getting into the inflatable, they propelled it through the channel, mainly by pushing on the side walls to save the battery.

Moving along the side of the stack was difficult, for petulant short waves were throwing them and the towed raft up against the rough rock, creating audible scraping noises as the fabric was being abraised. The paddles were also useful for fending off the rock wall. They reached the channel and the arch intact. The gap between the water and the apex of the arch was much the same as before; what was different now was the surge. It was quite lively and they thought it might be possible to be flattened against the roof of the entrance which could have catastrophic consequences. It was grim, but they pressed on and, lying supine in the inflatable with the raft behind, passed inside, twice being smashed violently up to the roof with the powerful and irresistible thrust of sheer power.

They were inside and in relative calm. It was as if the stack's presence had calmed the sea and though the cavern's inside pool was rising and falling in slow motion, it had a calming quality. Mother stack will look after you, it soothed. Not a bloody hope in hell of that, Derek thought. They would be cast out like keel hauled sailors to be shredded on the Torridonian sandstone battlements.

Chapter 26

They moved into top gear. There could be no indecision, no farting around. The now battle-worn inflatable and raft were tethered at the steps and only essentials were taken above.

They had just arrived at the top of the steps when Michelle sent her routine call. This was acknowledged by Derek and both, using headlamps and two floodlights, had managed to take up everything they needed, making a pile of the bags inside the stone door.

After frenzied work, it took about half the number of bags to hold all the remaining pieces within the stack. Some spare bags were used as padding for the swords and a stunning diamond studded tiara which seemed to dance in the headlamp beams as if rejoicing in its impending freedom. Both men went back into the chambers to make a final check. Derek gave a thumbs up and they moved out without a word. Indeed, nothing had been said since a stream of invective when they were crushed into the roof of the arch. Duncan, holding on to the lowering rope with one hand and the bundle of empty bags in the other, descended in minutes. He threw these into the bottom of the raft and gave the rope a tug. This was the signal and one after the other bags came down, free of the steps, and swung into the raft. The last was indicated by the top end of the rope snaking down after it. Duncan secured the cargo with the retaining net as Derek joined him. They were still using headlamps, grateful that both the NVGs and the lamps were waterproof. They would be further tested at the exit from the stack, Derek thought.

The raft hadn't yet been lowered deeper into the water due to the lighter load, but as they approached what was still showing of the arch, they had doubts if it would make it. They both moved their headlamps down round their necks – the NVGs were folded flat on their chests. When they reached the arch, the fluctuation of the water level was much more pronounced and they lay back in the watery bed of the inflatable awaiting their chance, hoping the raft would follow it, but as a last resort it could be lowered and hauled through. This would take valuable time. For the present, the motor was switched off for they didn't want a situation where it could be driving them like a wedge between its floor and the roof of the arch. For several minutes they watched the varying water level to see if there was a pattern in gap height. It appeared that every fifth pulse gave more headroom and they agreed to go for this. Both realised that the inflatable could be a death trap, for if they got trapped under the roof for more than a few minutes they could be drowned, being unable to get out from under the encircling outer tubes.

"Let's go," Derek yelled, switching the motor on full and madly pushing up against the rock as they scraped along. He felt the blood running from his face as he was pressed against the rough, sharp surface. Duncan, who was going feet first, fared little better. Suddenly Derek's head came out from beneath, just as the water was rising and, sitting up, he thrust both feet upward against the top of the arch. Duncan was pulling like mad with bloody fingers on the rock where possible, as there weren't many upside down holds. Derek got a grip of his friend's ankles and adjusted both boots above on the edge of the arch while leaning backwards. It took all his strength to pull the inflatable and his friend free. Like a stubborn champagne cork it suddenly popped out of the arch and he fell backwards into the bows, breathless and spitting out salt water. His headlamp, which he had slid up on his forehead, shone down on Duncan. He looked like an overgrown Moses combining baptism while reclining in a pneumatic cradle.

The current from the channel was now stronger and they realised that they would have to work quickly to extricate the raft. They pulled on its tethering rope and knew that it had reached the edge of the other side of the arch. They waited, tense. The water was going down again from its highest point. Derek shouted to his friend who was still trying to recover some of his dignity.

"Start pulling, Duncan. If it gets stuck we will just wait until the water goes down again. Everything is in the bags, anyhow,"

Sure enough, it was on the next low pulse that they managed to extricate it. Other than being filled with water, it appeared undamaged, with only a few strands of the cargo net torn. They now reverted to NVGs.

Things were getting agitated and they quickly made adjustments and got under way. Derek put the inflatable on full thrust which didn't appear to have a great deal of effect, probably due to the quantity of water inside the raft. By combining paddling, they did make progress, but it was getting choppy and their craft was shipping water. Also it was too dangerous now to go alongside the rock wall as there was the probability of smashing into it, yet by keeping to more open water there was the risk of capsizing.

Eventually, after a hazardous passage, they approached the mouth of the geo. It looked forbidding with angry waves snapping at its portals and the space behind could have doubled for the entrance to Hades. There was trouble in tethering the raft to its boulder, but they found another, further in, which was providential. Here they managed to pump out some water, as there had been no opportunity on the way round to do this. They used the motor to get up the geo's channel and were beyond caring about damage to the dinghy. After a few bumps they were alongside their rib. It felt like home, impervious to anything that nature could throw at it. The inflatable, which had also proved to be a reliable companion, was hauled aboard and as Duncan cast off Jack's ropes, Derek got the silent motor running. Duncan took up position to ward off rock walls and boulders on the exit.

When they reached the raft there was a problem getting alongside as there wasn't enough room now that it was further into the channel. Duncan got it untied and pushed it out, closer to the entrance. Derek squeezed alongside. Even in the shelter of the geo the raft was bucking. Duncan, who had clambered aboard, passed the bags into the rib. This was done quickly and Derek hurriedly placed them in the centre of the deck and lashed them down. Once it was relieved of its remaining water, the raft was tied back to back with the inflatable. No sooner had this been done than there was a call from Michelle on their dedicated frequency.

"St Kilda, force 8."

Derek pressed the transmit button on the top of one of his belt pouches.

"St Kilda, force 8. Did you receive that, Duncan?" The big man nodded.

"Should we wait for a bit in here?"

"I think that's the better option."

Then they heard the distinctive note of gas turbines, an eerie sound in the confines of the rock hole. They were getting closer and louder.

"It must be Banderoski," Duncan spat out. "He probably located the geo from a chart, for they knew that Jack must have had a boat, but how the hell did they get that chopper going again so soon?"

"They must be using NVGs," Derek stated over their intercom.

Now the noise was deafening, ricocheting from the confines of their cave and they got a momentary glimpse of the machine as it passed.

"Get your rifle, Duncan, and my UZI and 45, also the launcher with a heat seeking round in the spout as a last resort. Also that hand searchlight in the nose locker. We may have to shoot our way out of here for there's not enough cover and the lamp may provide some dazzle for the pilot. They could hear the helicopter returning along the cliff. They must have realised that they had overshot the geo and wouldn't make that mistake a second time. Duncan put the weapons in their now open flight cases in front of Derek. He held his AK-47 as if it was a toy.

The helicopter was closer on this pass. It was difficult to judge precisely due to the echo. The two men had nowhere to go and had to stand their ground, so to speak. They held their breath and then saw the nose of a Eurocopter Fennec slowly come into view. With their NVGs the two men could see extruded light emanating from the engine. The passenger doors were off and on each side a man was attached to a safety sling with their feet on the landing skids. Both had sub machine guns. They didn't have NVGs, but the pilot had, and now the aircraft was fitted with a powerful Night Sun searchlight. Duncan saw the danger immediately and with a single shot shattered it just as it was lighting up. It was uncanny: there was just this flash as the lamp cut in, then it was dead. This was followed by a volley of automatic fire, but the machine wheeled away.

"Good shooting, Duncan."

"Oh, I get a lot of practice these days with the clay pigeons, but I am quite pleased considering it wasn't my shotgun."

"I don't think that we can hold out here, Duncan, and I suspect that the Eurocopter can't hang about long either. If they realize they can get a shot from above where the SAR boys first spotted that bit of tarpaulin, we've had it."

"I see what you mean."

"How about sneaking out on one engine? There would be almost no wake. Anyhow, this choppy sea will hide it and we could cover up with the camouflage nets. We would be difficult to spot even with good radar, which I don't think they have. I didn't see any aerial on the aircraft when it was in the barn, did you?"

"No, I didn't. It seems a good scheme. Let's cover up."

"I'll give Michelle a call in ornithological code. 'St Kilda to St Kilda advise force 8. Manx Shearwater returning to burrows."

"I heard your message, Derek. She may understand. I did."

It didn't take long to cover the engines and deck area of the rib and the net could be pulled up over the console and controls if necessary.

"There's just one more thought, Duncan. Suppose that the chopper was here as a recce and that a replacement rib is on its way."

"Possible, but when you think of it, why go in darkness to the stack when you can go during the day. We had to adopt our scheme to avoid detection from both the good and the bad. That does not apply to them. They could just park nearby with one of them left in the rib and the others could clean out the stack double quick. They don't know that they are too late."

"Don't you think Banderoski was out for revenge for our raid and the only place where he thought he could find us was at the stack?"

"In that case he was right."

The rib glided out of the geo in complete darkness. The wind had got up and the sea felt as if it was looking for an argument. There were no stars, but the NVGs still functioned, but lacked clarity. Derek took the rib up to fifteen knots and set the auto pilot on the bearing to the boatyard.

There was no visible wake. When they got out of the shelter of Sanday, the westerly flexed its muscles and buffeted the port side of the rib. Derek looked at the instruments. They were about half way home now and echo sounder was indicating 180 metres. They were crossing the North-South Trench between Sanday and the mainland.

Over their headsets came a terse warning.

"St Kilda, force 8, imminent."

Immediately, they heard the shrill whine of turbines again. The noise emanated from straight ahead, very low. Derek cut in the other three engines and pulled the throttle back as far as it would go. The rib rose as if released from a carrier's catapult and rose above the waves, appearing as if it would collide with the oncoming helicopter, but it must have been at least four metres below. The pilot was obviously startled for he pulled back the stick and rose spectacularly. The two men in the rib saw pin points of light from automatic fire.

"Give me that launcher, Duncan. It's them or us...!"

"Them," Duncan's voice came over Derek's earpiece and above the roar of the engines. Duncan placed the loaded weapon at Derek's feet. He throttled back to reduce the noise for they had to get as much warning as possible. Just then Michelle cut in over the RT.

"St Kilda, force 8 from west."

"The bastard going to get us from the rear," Duncan shouted.

In an instant Derek grabbed the rocket launcher and waited until he could hear the Fennec. It was getting close.

"No point in waiting with a weapon like this, Duncan he shouted. "It would even find it at the back of the geo, but get another missile, just in case."

He squeezed the trigger and a jet of flame leapt out of the rear end like a mini dragster. In a millisecond it homed in on the radiated heat of the turbo jet engines. The ensuing explosion was momentous and lit up the entire Sound. As if in slow mode this white plume lit the gathering clouds and a blast of hot air rocked the rib, almost throwing them on the deck. Then there was a silence as if nature had paused in fright.

Inevitably, the weather took over as if annoyed that it had been upstaged. Derek recorded the GPS position and slowly turned the rib round, careful to avoid any debris, but there wasn't any. Nothing. Instinctively, he kept to windward. He knew that this was no ordinary detonation. There was nothing, not a single floating fragment to be seen. It was as if a great hot hand had grabbed the aircraft and pulled it into the deeps.

"What do you know?" Duncan muttered, amazed. The ribs engines were just quietly ticking over. "I've never seen a chopper disappear like that, ever, and I've seen a few go down.

But it does remind me of the Bealach Uiske explosion," he recalled, "an all enveloping, blinding whiteness and that searing heat. You know, I never mentioned it, but there was a question of radiation after the Bealach big bang. Both the doc and myself were cleared though. They said if radio activity had been present it was possibly negated by the blizzard – which just about did the job instead."

"I think it was a Depleted Uranium rocket, Duncan, and all evidence has disappeared into one of the deepest patches of Scottish coastal water. It makes me wonder about that missile. Just think what Depleted Uranium can do, especially when there is no armour to devour, nothing, not even any local oxygen." He continued. "I was curious about those rockets, Duncan. The label was in Russian so I couldn't read it. I know that I asked for 'high explosive', but not that explosive."

"It's all the same in the end," Duncan observed, philo-sophically, placing his rifle back in its case. "It was kill or be killed and I feel that we have avenged Jack's demise and saved the remains of the Templar hoard."

"How do you think the chopper found us, Duncan?"

"I think it was trained luck," his friend replied. "That Fennec is, was, an uprated military machine, even the paint colour. That light colour denotes Thermal and Radar Signature Management, clever stuff. Also a bit of Scottish mist doesn't go amiss. The pilot would have facilities for searching Grid Pattern and it was only a matter of time before he got us."

"Thank goodness Michelle's a quick thinker. Come to think of it, I'd better let her know that we are not vaporised. She will be worried – I know we were!" He pressed the transmit button on his hand set. St Kilda to St Kilda, Manx Shearwater completed."

Slowly, they turned round for the boatyard, both deep in thought. As they approached, Derek said, "Duncan, that chopper has vanished without trace, its cinders in very deep water. Mother nature with cloud and darkness provided further cover. The story for Michelle and all others…?"

"…It just seemed to explode as it approached – end of chapter."

"Roger."

Instead of tying up at the jetty, they positioned the rib above the ramp launching trolley, which was now under-water.

Michelle's voice came clearly from above, out of the darkness.

Chapter 27

"Hello there."

"We're both OK, Michelle. Give us a few minutes to pull the rib out and thanks for saving our bacon. We have the goodies!"

"As long as you are both intact I don't give a Fuck about the bloody rib or the hoard!"

"I never thought that I would ever hear that," Derek called.

"Well, I mean it."

After giving Michelle a hug, difficult with NVGs on, Derek went to the winch controls and in minutes the rib crept up the ramp to beneath the overhead hoist. It was then lifted off the trolley with its dedicated slings. The trolley was returned to the top of the ramp, its place of residence. The sea door was lowered for the last time and the lights switched on. Still no one spoke and the bags were transferred into the rear of the Range Rover and the hired equipment back into the rib. Duncan raised it to about five metres. When the two men took off their dry suits Michelle spoke. She had been silent but was now full of expectation.

"I have replaced the hard drives in the camera module. You can view the used ones back at the house when you wish."

"Thanks," Derek responded, hugging her again. "You did an amazing job."

"I can second that," Duncan agreed. "Some quick thinking, girl. Let's get back. I'm hungry enough to eat Mrs Mathieson for breakfast. But there are things to do first."

The vehicle was unloaded at the garage. It was now light.

There was a feeling of completion round the breakfast table. A relief that they had come in from the cold. It was most tangible in Michelle for in the past few days she had lacked her usual sparkle. It was as if she felt that she was going to lose something – if not everything. The two men, who had lived for years as if there was no tomorrow, showed little sign, but of course they were individuals who didn't advertise emotions.

Even Mrs Mathieson seemed more sprightly and her high unsaturated fat platters of all day breakfasts were mandatory. It was her blow for common sense, Michelle heard her mutter under her breath.

The housekeeper asked Duncan with barely a trace of sarcasm in her voice.

"Did you see any birds on your travels last night? It's gae rough now."

"We did before it got bad, but I think we have completed our survey."

"The Lord be thanked." She announced this in her usual way without any innuendo and as if she meant it. After she left the room Michelle spluttered with laughter.

"Good God, Duncan, you two. Why don't you say what you mean?"

"Why not?", Derek echoed. "That would spoil our fun."

"Ah well," Duncan sighed. "That may be, but it's the way

things are done in the Highlands. One doesn't like to offend; it's an old Celtic trait."

"I think that you will be relieved of your wayward guests shortly, Duncan, once we get some semblance of order in the contents of your garage. How long do you think this will take, Michelle, cataloguing etc., not cleaning? Which we couldn't do anyway?"

"I would think a few days and I'd better e-mail a selection of pics to the National Museum of Scotland as I mentioned all historical finds have to be sent there and the British Museum informed. It will give them an idea of what to expect and I must check that there is no salt water damage. It will take some time to individually bag, photograph, number and box. I would imagine the British Museum will ask to send some of their experts north to participate with the cataloguing."

"Despite everything," Duncan stated, "I think that we treated the goods with kid gloves considering. I've used those black Kevlar submersible bags for years and always found them a hundred per cent."

"I must get the address from you for they would be excellent for our digs and marine work."

"Sure, I'll give it to you. He's an illicit arms dealer on the West Bank."

"Ask a stupid question…" She made a face at him, but still looked remarkably attractive.

Derek spoke. "Before we continue, Michelle, tell us what happened on your front last night."

"Well," she started, abstractly inspecting her broken nail. "I don't think it was as entertaining as a MacGillvery-Hawthorne episode, but what it lacked in humour it made up in drama. I'll be as brief as possible. First, I experienced limitations with the camera unit. Once that damp cloud came in there was an obvious drop in definition in the duel system, even when enhanced. I lost you on several occasions – that rib is remarkable; on your return trip from the geo you were mostly invisible."

"We had our stealth camouflage net on," Duncan told her.

"I must get the address for one of those too," she mused. "No, on second thoughts I won't bother you. To get back to the tale in hand. The St Kilda code seemed to work well, but your message about that blasted Manx Shearwater almost stumped me."

"Well, it was your warning about the approaching force 8 that saved our lives. We almost ended at the bottom of the Atlantic resembling bullet-holed sponges."

"I'm glad that I have my uses, I sometimes wonder. Now, when I have doubts I'll think of an Atlantic sponge – they're very rare. I had a bit of luck when the chopper found you on its way back. I didn't know exactly where you were, but I had your previous GPS plots on the screen and I knew that you would be going slowly to prevent the rib's wake giving you away. I also guessed roughly where you should be and as the chopper was coming in a direct line with the camera position, I wasn't picking up the engine heat on infra red initially. Then someone in the cabin switched on a light, a torch or something, just for an instant, but I had a fix. That was when I gave the warning. On your first encounter with the helicopter I could see clearly the machine gun flashes, then suddenly they seemed to be firing up in the air."

"They were," Duncan informed her. "Derek gave the rib full throttle towards the oncoming helicopter, which was very low, and it must have taken the pilot with his NVG by surprise!"

"What happened then" Derek asked Michelle. "This is intriguing."

"That's the strange thing," she confessed. "Everything went dead; it was utter darkness."

Derek told her. "The Fennec found us. That was just after your warning. Eugene, who we think was the pilot, probably used a Grid Search System. We were expecting to be shot to bits, then it exploded in a white light. There wasn't even an item of flotsam left. That's the reason the camera packed in. There's a circuitry cutout."

There was a pause, then Duncan looked at her gravely.

"We both feel that this puts an end to the matter and at least gives some retribution for the loss of Jack Rippon, for they were responsible for his death."

"Another thing," Derek announced. "As Duncan's friend, Torkil MacKenzie, owns the island of Sanday, it is he, who will have a right for a percentage of the Treasure Trove.

"What a story," Michelle breathed. "It's like something from the *Arabian Nights*. However, now under new rulings the decision comes under the Scottish Treasure Trove Unit, though this should not effect the amount paid for the find.

"More like the 'Templar Nights' as it was found in the hours of darkness."

"Not again," Duncan moaned.

"As my observations are not appreciated," Derek gave one of his grins, "back to the future. I will ask for the rib to be collected later today, but I suggest we leave the camera running until this storm blows over. It will be fascinating to witness any further interest in the stack. Some of the remaining divers out from Dubh Craig Estate may have ideas."

"When on the subject, Michelle," Duncan asked, "did you ever come across any medieval vases for sale on the Web?"

"I'm still keeping an eye on it," she responded.

"Looking to the future," Duncan asked, "how do we get the loot down to the museum?"

"Well, they can arrange collection," Michelle replied, "or we could hire a van and drive it down."

"I would prefer that," Duncan stated. "You, Derek?"

"I agree. We've done things thus far and I feel we should deliver the goods. We could take it down, Michelle, and return for my car."

"That would suit me as I have endless things to deal with on my 'croft'," Duncan agreed. "Torkil is due back soon and I'd better thank him for the use of the boatyard and break the big news gently. He will be able to implement some of his ideas, hopefully. We can all get together when you come back up."

"After I make some phone calls, I'll grab a few hours' sleep." Derek gave a yawn. "How about you two?"

"Yes." Michelle stood up.

"Yes, too," Duncan agreed.

Derek got through to the rib suppliers before he went to bed. The truck would be back at the boatyard at 3 am the following morning. They had only three hours' sleep and Duncan and Derek went down to the boatyard to complete their withdrawal. They checked the overnight footage, but there was nothing of interest and they realised that Michelle's observation on the bad weather capabilities was correct; cloud, rain and spray certainly had a detrimental effect on the quality of the recordings.

"We must have a look at those hard drives she took back, Duncan. It will be interesting, as the good book says, '...for now we see through a glass, darkly'."

"Corinthians 13, verse 4."

"You always surprise me, you old bugger," Derek laughed, "but I can just see you, creeping like a snail to bible class."

"You had better watch out, Colonel, you'll trip up one of these days."

The low loader arrived on time and the complete withdrawal of the rib and equipment went without a hitch and Duncan and Derek locked up the boathouse in exactly the state they had found it.

Over breakfast Derek said to Michelle, "I can give you a hand for a couple of hours, Duncan has laird's work to do."

"Great," she responded. "I see why you were enthusiastic about those swords. I had a quick look at them. They are really magnificent."

"If I wanted to keep a particular sample of this collection," Duncan, who had almost finished his meal looked pensive, "it would be one of those."

"I would go for the other one," Derek rejoined and hurriedly added, "of course, for both of us, Michelle."

"Don't worry," she replied. "I wouldn't dream of taking your toys, but I had my eye on that priceless necklace, though I don't desire these things. I recall similar emotions when I uncovered a rare Egyptian gold bangle."

"You would have to be an artistic anchorite to live with such a bauble, even if it is a work of art," Duncan observed. "It would have to be locked away and you would be in constant fear that it would be stolen. I prefer my simple life, getting my kicks from scenery and seascapes in this part of the world."

"I can understand that, Duncan." Michelle was thoughtful. "I have a hankering for such wild places, too."

"Before we do anything else, I'd like to see the discs, Michelle," Derek suggested.

"I'll go and get them and take them to the office."

She ran at double speed to the first of the saved sequences from leaving the boatyard in the dark, then the remainder of the operation. There was little to see clearly, for the bad weather and near total darkness rendered the surveillance almost useless. There was a blinding flash of light, then blackness."

"I see what you meant, Michelle, we were lucky that the camera unit worked properly when required!"

"It seems to be a hundred per cent again," Michelle told them. "I managed to rig up a relay from the boatyard to the spare module here and the only craft shown since I changed over the drives, was a small fishing boat heading north."

"I think that we have finished with the camera now," Derek concluded. "We can pack it up and send it home."

Clearing up the signs of their occupation of the camera's rocky headland didn't take long and the nocturnal collection of the rib went, as they expected, smoothly.

However, it was a further week before Michelle, Derek and Duncan managed to establish some order with the contents of the stack. Eventually, everything was photographed, labelled and packaged in special fibreboard crates, 420 items. A large hired van was delivered and the following day Michelle and Derek set off with their precious cargo.

A year later, Michelle and Derek were in the Verdon Gorge in southern France. They were staying at a holiday home belonging to her father. It had been a farm, then an equestrian business. It was in a superb setting beneath the limestone peaks. Michelle was relaxing on a deck chair and, looking up, she saw Derek coming down the trail.

"Hi, did you do it?"

He gave a thumbs down. "Too bloody hot," he called when he got closer.

"I'll get you a cold lime and lemon," she offered and dashed into the house.

By the time she came back he was sitting beneath the

umbrella. He was dressed in shorts and rock boots and his day sack was beside him.

"Thanks," he said, gratefully taking a long gulp. "How do you look so cool?"

"I've got more sense than to attempt a route in this heat."

"I reached the same conclusion," he confessed, "and abseiled off. These new climbs are too hard. You have to be a gecko."

"You haven't got the build, or suckers on your feet either," she teased. "And whilst I was lazing here I was thinking of cooler places: Inverstack. We have loose ends to discuss with our partners. Duncan suggested as much in his last e-mail."

He looked at her and smiled. He seemed much more relaxed now, she thought, probably more so than she ever remembered.

"Today or tomorrow?"

"Tomorrow, I have to get some clothes on."

"I wouldn't do that if I were you. It will spoil the fun."

Chapter 28

They arrived at Inverstack in a car hired at Dalcross Airport, Inverness. The journey reminded them of when he picked her up off the train almost a year ago to the day. On the route north and west, Beinn Wyvis was squat and white as if the late Queen Victoria had shed her mourning clothes for a white petticoat beneath. Dawdling tourists and obese caravans were causing the seasonal thrombosis with their 'take in everything' at zero speed.

"You shouldn't get so impatient, Derek. They are enjoying themselves." She gave a laugh. "Here, have a new sweet, a pink striped ball. I got them at the airport. They are supposed to be good for stress."

"Shit," he retorted.

Duncan was waiting for them, for they had given him a call when passing through the village.

"My goodness, when you last arrived here I was singed to the eyebrows, but look at you both, you appear over-baked."

"Oh, it's good to be back, Duncan." Michelle ran over to him and gave him a big hug, then looked at him closely.

"Yes, you look back to normal – at least, as normal as ever you were."

"I see that Hawthorne's humour is rubbing off on you, girl, you'll be quoting some corny text any minute. Come ben the hoose, as they say in these parts. Mrs Mathieson is all excited that you are back."

"I hope that you told her, Duncan, that we haven't come to take you off chasing wild birds."

"Or geese," Derek suggested.

"Oh, she has the advantage of the second sight, Colonel."

"Does that mean that she has a second look at you to see if you are telling the truth?"

It was the following afternoon that Torkil MacKenzie-Baron joined them for a 'pow-wow', as he termed their meeting. He greeted them.

"Ah," he cleared his throat, "sorry that we didn't have much time to chat when I returned. I feel indebted to all three of you; it was a remarkable find." He turned to Michelle. "I understand that you are an expert in such things."

"Just a run of the mill marine archaeologist," she confessed.

They were all sitting around a small drawing-room adjoining the lounge. Torkil's ancestors had lived in the area for generations. Though in his late forties, he had served in the army on active service, 'in the ranks of a real regiment', as he liked to put it, before they were all put in the melting pot of government bureaucracy and renamed the Regiment of Scotland.

He knew a bit about Duncan's earlier career and there was the tittle-tattle from colleagues where, when the title Special Services comes up, everyone shuts up. He was of medium build and looked fit and very much with it. His face was rather florid, probably due to the blast of fresh air which he was subjected to in his vintage compressor Bentley.

"How your son Torkil?"

"Loves it, out there unlike many crofters who left here all those years ago during the potato famine. He's lucky and had a good job to go to, Duncan."

"I haven't had much of a chance to speak with Derek and Michelle, Torkil," Duncan announced, "so I will out-line what has been happening. You are aware of most of it." He looked out of the window at a buzzard which was lazily looking for a rabbit or perhaps a field mouse for a late lunch. "Legally, the treasure trove was found jointly by Derek, Michelle and myself and, as it was located within the stack, technically within Torkil's estate, we four will share a division of the valuation. The valuation of the trove will be accessed and divided equally between the four of us. There will be a formal document drawn up by the solici-tors, less the expenses of the operation, rental of your boat-yard, etc. Everyone happy with that?"

"I think that's very fair," Torkil agreed.

"Me, too," Derek echoed. "After all, it started as a hobby."

"Fine by me," Michelle said. "After all, it's my job."

"Well, that seems settled," Duncan announced. "Can you tell us what's the latest feed back from the museums, Michelle?"

"A year seems a long time," she replied, "but not for my work which deals in centuries. I gather that a provisional valuation will be publicly announced shortly from Edinburgh. I have no idea what this will be, but I am assured that it is one of the largest treasure troves in modern times and will run into many millions of pounds."

"Good grief," Torkil spluttered. "I never imagined. I

must go back home and tell my good lady. She will have a heart attack."

"I presume you mean that it's 'good news', Torkil, and I suggest that you should convey that to the Honourable Margaret gently. We would hate to lose her."

"You are a wag, Duncan." He waved a finger at him. "Oh, before I go, Michelle, you were interested in the boat-yard. I will have a word with you before you leave if that is the case. As a matter of fact there is outline planning for a house on the site, Duncan can fill you in on that."

Once Torkil noisily departed, they moved into the main lounge and Duncan suggested that he gave a full account to his two friends of his investigations since they departed. They settled in the armchairs and both looked expectantly at him.

"There have been several developments," he started. "First the Islander. I contacted a Scottish university that specialises in satellite imagery and in fact paid them a visit, going through dozens of orbits covering the Glen Uiske area about the time of the explosion in the blizzard. Eventually, I found what I was looking for. That aircraft, the twin Islander, flew east the day before Dave and I were on the climb. It must have crashed then and was only blown up after Eugene salvaged their share of the treasure which was probably en-route for the black market."

"I have further news on that," Michelle interrupted. "I traced a couple of days ago, you know about this Derek, that some of the items from that crash are to be auctioned in Moscow. From the illustrations, I would say that they are from the stack."

"It looks as if Eugene's pals are pursuing that transaction," Duncan stated. "I was speaking further with my friend who drives an SAR Merlin. You may recall that I asked him about choppers sneaking about the Minch."

"And?" Derek prompted.

"Well, John, the pilot, overflew the Dubh Craig hangar and the doors were open. He got a good view of the helicopter, just before the doors were closed. John was interested in this scenario as there wasn't any record of a Fennec Eurocopter based in the Outer Hebrides. As he was at one time in RAF Intelligence, he went on to the old boy network to find out anything on Eugene Banderoski. Apparently, after university years he became an outstanding pilot in the Russian military as well as a marine historian and salvage expert. His employees tended to be ex-Russian Special Services and Spetsnaz who don't let protocol stand in their way. Word has got about that he was liable to be arrested had he returned to Russia, the same goes for his chief mechanic."

"Well, I see that you have been busy, Duncan. What's happened to the galleon salvage ploy?"

"It has apparently been wound up. No mention of Eugene or his crew. I gather that a solicitor in Inverness has been asked by a property agent in Gorky to put the estate on the market, some relative of Eugene's, I suppose. There's one other thing I have been discussing with Torkil about the boatyard. He would be willing to sell it together with quite a lump of land at an extremely attractive price, but he mentioned another part of his estate, only about ten miles from here."

"Tell me," Michelle prompted, excitedly.

"Well, it's on a fantastic bay and is a de-crofted property with about four hundred acres, all of the old Common Grazings."

"Can you show me on a map?" she asked.

"I can do better than that. I went back to the spot for I had only been there once before and it's quite remarkable. It has a single track road leading to it," he continued. "I racked my brains over my own property, but Inverstack ground is mainly stalking and mountains – up and down, whereas ... I'd better give you the Gaelic translation of the name: 'House of the Great Ocean'. Mind you," he smiled, "it will need a bit of work. I made up a MacGillvery portfolio for you and have even some movie footage. When do you want to see it?"

"Immediately, you bastard. You're stringing me along."

"Come into the office. I can assure you that this place is the jewel in the crown as far as seascapes, sand and machair go. And good old Torkil will part with it for a give away price – I think he has taken a fancy for you. He feels also that he will be forever in our debt! He said it's the least he can do!"

Hamish MacInnes is an international mountaineer who has written thirty books, including three novels, several have been translated in various languages. He is also a world authority on mountain Rescue and his work, "International Mountain Rescue Handbook" has been in constant print since 1972.
Also, he is the designer of the MacInnes mountain rescue stretchers which have evacuated thousands of injured climbers world wide and was a leading pioneer in modern ice climbing. In his spare time Hamish has advised on major feature films such as *The Eiger Sanction*, *Highlander*, *The Living Daylights*, *Five Days one Summer*, *The Mission* etc. There have been many expeditions during this period including yeti hunting and four trips to Amazonia, one climbing Mt Roraima, Conan Doyle's Lost World and the other three searching for Inca Treasure. His interest in Templar treasure stems from information obtained when writing a guide book on the Highlands. Hamish lives in Glencoe after having climbed on five continents.